AF441128

TPS PUBLISHING

Warning

This book contains sexually explicit scenes, homoerotica, a MM relationship, and adult language, which may not be to the liking for some readers. It is intended for sale and the entertainment to adults only, as defined by the laws of the country in which you made your purchase. Please store your files wisely, where they cannot be accessed by under-aged readers.

Muse Me Only

Tarian P.S.

Gay-MM / Erotic Romance / Painter & Dancer Theme / Muse to Lovers / Even Introverts Need Love / Saucy Meet-Cute / Falling for your Muse / Fast Burn / Extreme Heat / Revenge is Sweet with a Partner to Support You / Believing in You / Wrong Fight to Pick / Love Heals Riffs / HEA

Xherdan Chantal is an artist still trying to find his place among the masters of color. He's a rather independent soul, working at the New York Metropolitan Museum, who lends no time to pretending to be anything he's not or be involved in anyway other than to stimulate his muse.

However, when a local pole dancer sneaks a shoulder-mount-to-flying-half-flag maneuver into his life, managing to seduce far more than Xherdan's muse, he's not sure how to put it all into perspective. Then again, painting is Xherdan's artistic magic, not words. So, while poetic prose may have failed him, he still enjoys exploring this new sensation with loyal attention that sets Sreven above the rest of the world that's only purpose is to feed his muse. Rather, Sreven becomes the living motion and breath of his muse.

But there's just one fight a lover should never pick with an artist.

TRADEMARK ACKNOWLEDGEMENTS

<u>ARTIST :</u>

> Libor Sostak – Artist
> Petra Krausová – Artist
> Petra Řehořová – Artist
> Michael Young – Artist
> Norman Rockwell – Artist
> Channing Tatum – Actor
> Mark Arian – Artist
> Ennion – Artist

<u>DANCERS :</u>

> Gary Jetter – Dancer
> Alex Chu – Dancer
> Josh Taylor – Dancer
> Mikhail Baryshnikov – Dancer
> Yanis Marshall – Dancer/Choreographer

<u>MUSIC :</u>

> Song: Patience by Suduaya
> Song: Vengeance by Zack Hemsey
> Song: World Without End by Brand X Music
> Song: Your Heart's a Mess by Gotye
> Sting – Singer
> Song: Deeper Into You by Johnny Hazzard

<u>MISCELLANEOUS :</u>

Cirque Du Soleil – Circus/ Artistic Performance Show
Marco Marco – Mens Designer Clothing
Christian Louboutins – Designer Shoe wear
Gatorade© – Sportsdrink by PepsiCo
Energizer Bunny^{T} - Trademark of Energizer
Advil - Advil©
Alan Watts - Philosopher
Tommy Bahamas cologne for men
Book Character: Cujo by Stephen King
'Kinetic Rain' Sculpture by Artist Jussi Angeleva
Quote: "Why is a raven like a writing desk?" ~ Alison in
Wonderland by Lewis Carroll

DEDICATION

To Talon, because not a day goes by I don't feel your
absence. ~Your twin

To Damir,

who was my role model for Xherdan. Because over the
years you have shown me how even an Ass can love with
immeasurable passion and loyalty when the right
person for them comes along. And to Ethan, who has
shown me it's how we bond with our flaws included that
makes love stronger. Thank you for letting me see into
your world with you and your husband.

TABLE OF CONTENT

Muse Me Only

TARIAN P.S.

Muse Me Only

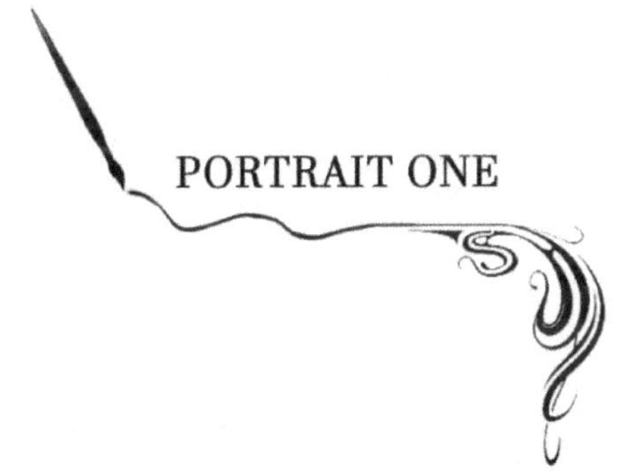

PORTRAIT ONE

The veins in his arm nearly popped through his skin just seconds after gripping the pole. In the same instance, his feet came up off the floor and he lifted his legs in a slow movement, as he forced each to fan out, and continued lifting before turning in a slow aerial pirouette until he had twisted all the way around. His pointed toes hovered above the stage and left his body in such a contorted manner that he likely just killed himself. *Poor soul.* He could have at least let me paint him then fuck him before he'd committed pole-dancer suicide.

And then— as if he'd heard my thoughts giving him new reason to live, those legs flew up into a series of movements that a smartass like me could only describe as part dance, part flip-flop, part Olympic pole vault; leaving out all the eloquence and amazement that went along with what I was seeing. It was exciting for sure, but it didn't *excite*-excite me. Not the way perhaps it was meant to as the venue's purpose would suggest with a name like *The Pumping Station*. Then again, I wasn't entirely sure. I mean, were we supposed to get erections while watching this? Because I didn't feel it. I was enthralled, yes— much in the same way as watching Mikhail Baryshnikov in a solo performance. Okay, for him, I did get hard.

Go ahead and laugh about my ballet reference. But there was something astonishing about watching the Russian dance-extraordinaire leap up in the air with a triple axel twist that ended in a pinwheel kick before landing on his toes like he was a butterfly on steroids.

Did I lose you with that one? Of course, I did, because while I was talking about the amazing muscular body of one of the world's most talented male ballet dancers in his ability to land as softly as an angel's feather, you were busy thinking about man-bulges in tights, and you missed the purpose of my visual. Nevertheless, I remember, some years ago, I was still a young boy when I accompanied my mother and father to the ballet. Quite ostensibly, it may have been the very moment when I experienced my first boyhood erection. An experience which started me down the path that would lead me to the self-realization that men turned me on far more than women did. For just when the symphony music kicked into its first bridge of the rhythmic theme, suddenly, this god in black tights and bare skin came leaping out from stage left. Champagne blonde hair flipped wildly around Baryshnikov's face. Muscles bulging in his back, arms, and thighs that accentuated every flexed move, both smooth and snapping.

Unlike the others, Mikhail was both grace and godly-packed, corded muscles. Just like the young man I was watching now, the experience to observe still astounded me. Yet, unlike the rest of Pole-Dancer's audience, who wore lust-filled faces, it was not making me horny. Now, had the man been standing here before me with that gleaming smile of his? I'd have had a whole 'nother reaction. That tanned face, hair that was most likely a dark blonde or sandy brown— hard to tell since it was buzzed down to the scalp. Even his whiter-than-winter smile did something to me. Awakened my Muse and perhaps as a sideshow, made me want to go all Tarzan on him, toss him over my shoulder, and climb the highest tree to make mad monkey love with him. Ape sound-effects and all. Okay, so not really— sex, yes— but minus the monkey effects.

The show ended when my pole dancer's feet returned to the stage. He released the pole and sprung his arms out with fingers splayed, palm up. He surprised me when a professional dancer's etiquette showed in him when he bowed, and then the lights went dark. Had I just watched him perform in the Cirque du Soleil, I would have certainly had a marvelous hard-on.

Instead, the room filled with cattle calls and whistling. It was so anti-theatrical to what I'd just watched, it nearly made me sick to my stomach. I pulled out my wallet, leafed a few bills out and dropped them down on the table. I went as far as scribble a note on the napkin, threatening the waiter that one of those bills had best make it into the hands of the dancer, then took a picture of the napkin and the two fifties, and then made my way towards the door, walking and texting as I went. I know. It's a talent of mine, but then I was determined as a kid to be a champion of walking and chewing bubble gum at the same time, despite what my mother always said of me.

The text included the snapshot I'd just taken, and the recipient, Zane-the-bartender, waved to me from behind the bar as I passed and headed out the door. It's a lot of work but given I'm an introvert, I harbor trust issues so this is how I tip.

I stopped and stood just outside the club, letting the night greet me. The nostalgic expectation ripped from my grasp when a city bus careened by with a blast of black exhaust that belched out just as it passed. It choked any pleasantry I was hoping for from my thoughts and my lungs. Fuck, I hated the city and yet I never could bring myself to leave it. Which meant spending a good amount of money on vacations just so I could prevent my own poor soul's declining existence due to smog. But wouldn't death make my value sky rocket? Wouldn't my dear estranged parents love that? Then they could feign the Broadway act with cheap sentiments of how much they would ache from their loss of such a sweet boy, who'd gone astray, only to irretrievably lose his life before he could find his way back to their mountebank, loving administry, as if to have been awaiting for him all along.

I despise cheap sentiments— I doubt you wonder why.

Nevertheless, much to their chagrin, I am alive— a sour reminder of their failure to punch out yet another golden carbon copy. *'Please let me introduce to you my son, Winchester Thurmond the third. Or is it the fourth? Fifth? My, doesn't time fly— I didn't realize my wife had produced so many replicas of myself. Perhaps I should have filed for a patent.'* Insert droll fake laugh. Then father would go on to how his protégé sons had attended Yale— just like him. Went into the family business— just like him. Drove a Lotus— just like him. Because that's what families with too much wealth and stale old prestige do. Too groomed even for a Norman Rockwell painting. Bleached blonde wife with the perfecto nose job. Hampton house with a white picket fence. *Ad nauseam.* Oh, but let us not forget the pedigree Bichon Frise pet and their six healthy, strapping sons. What a disappointment I was as the unveiling of their seventh and final baby protégé.

Having survived the growing up years, two hours after receiving my graduate certificate in a high school auditorium, I was hurried off to college to be certifiably dumped off and tucked out of sight.

Never fear— this would not be the symbol of the end of my journey. From there, I went and hitch-hiked from Yale, all the way to the Art School of Juilliard where I would begin my journey to excel in the arts. Though, I admit once there, I couldn't make up my mind which medium I liked most, so I focused my major on the management and antiquity studies of art with a second in painting art form.

Not to forget myself standing out here on the streets alone, I headed down the sidewalk of that same city as my thoughts rummaged through my past. And the same question kept popping up: *how was it I'd had the insight to plan so smartly?*

From the age of a young sprite, I had learned how calculated my parent's reaction to everything and thus always planned my contingencies. Like Julliard, I knew they would eventually find me out; after all, I had no intentions of staying in the closet about it for too long— just like the other closet I had stepped out of, early in life. That big rainbow closest in which ninety percent of all gay men stand in for a time or more before walking out to be free. Nevertheless, even for that outing celebration, I planned—

I allowed them to catch me in the act, that is. And with a second cousin no less. Had him tied to my father's bed using their *secret kinkery* toys and I videotaped the entire scene. A sweet blackmail, I must say, if I ever conjured one up. In fact, if it hadn't been for that decadent note of success, I might not have ever gotten off. You know where I went with that brilliant mess, yes?

I'd found that once my cousin was all tied up, I was at a loss with what to do with him. The whole domineering, top thing, just didn't ravage me as it does for others. But oh, the look on my father's face. And mom? Tsk tsk— yet it was the added perk of vengeance that sweetened the pot for what she'd done to me mere days before. After exposing myself and my second cousin before them, in their own bedroom, mother dearest made haste to pardon me from her plotting— something about a sudden grave illness and I was unable to attend the date she had arranged with the daughter of one of her gal pals in her Bridge League. A dreadful hook-up offense she never repeated ever again.

But oh don't let me leave out the best part— my price for my indiscretions.

If they truly wanted to assure, I was to forever forget about the adventurous discovery of their naughty toybox under their bed, they had to release my inheritance from dear deceased grandmama ahead of schedule. *And they did.*

There was no stopping my shenanigans after that.

That's how I managed to plan my Yale intervention. It wasn't the business part of it that I was rebuking. I seemed to have a natural flair at that sort of wit. But business law and global funding was about as exciting as watching flies fuck. I'll pass, thank you very much.

I felt the smile creep across my face as my mind slowly ventured to that particular night when the closet doors of art were flung open with audacious grandeur. It was in my second year of art school when I accompanied my parents to the Metropolitan Museum of Art for one of many annual fundraisers, to which my parents were predictable contributors. It just so happened that at these fundraisers, one or two lucky budding local artists were often included in the myriads of delectable displays.

Like plates filled with petit fours, caviar, and hors d'oeuvres— there was a sampling-flavor for every fickle pallet. Each spotlighted on the floor with a corner display, and my parents never even suspected what was coming.

I was grinning like a sultry peacock with lascivious expectation. We rounded the corner, and there among a few paintings was a larger-than-life sculpture of a naked man, who coincidentally resembled my second cousin— the very one I was caught fucking with my cock seated as deep as my balls would let me go, right there on their bed all those years ago. But, I digress. Excuse my jaunt down that erotic memory lane; it is, after all, one of my favorite moments.

Where was I? Ah, yes. The museum.

Displayed amongst other artists' imaginings and the 3-D corporeal version of my ticket to freedom were several paintings of my works. All modern idolizations of the male form, along with a self-rendition, charcoal sketch of myself, working on one of my paintings— also naked. I may have embellished my cock a bit, but since when do men not? My father had recently upgrade the size of his cock— he now drives a Ferrari. So, in my display, I went for the gusto and drew a big meat-hanger between my legs. It's quite distracting, to say the least.

About the only thing that could tear one's eyes from my sketched cock was the whites of my mother's eyes, bugged all the way out. Or maybe the O shape of her ruby red lips. My mother— ever the fashion maven, always making sure her shoes and purse matched to perfection, found a way to match her goggling eyes and usually pinched WASPish mouth. Her mouth gaped so wide her chin practically hit the floor. *I doubt in the history of nineteen year-olds there had ever been such a victory as mine!*

I must have worn that gloating, prideful smirk for a week. I think that was also the time of my first phone camera selfie, give or take a few hundred more. My thumb was laboriously busy in that spectacular moment.

As I understood it, my father conducted a studious investigation of my whereabouts after that momentous stunt. He found out my stand-in at Yale was just some kid from the Harlem projects, getting a great education. And when I say poor, I mean I found a kid, with big-big dreams, living in the ghettos, flipping burgers. Which, my father let be when threatened with public humiliation as a cuckold Scrooge if he so much as stripped the young man a day of his gratuitous four-year scholarship. I also never heard from him or my mother again.

That was ten years ago.

My name is Xherdan Chantal. I am the lofty, waywardly lost gay son of a pragmatically wealthy Connecticut family of old Swiss money, and *this* is my story.

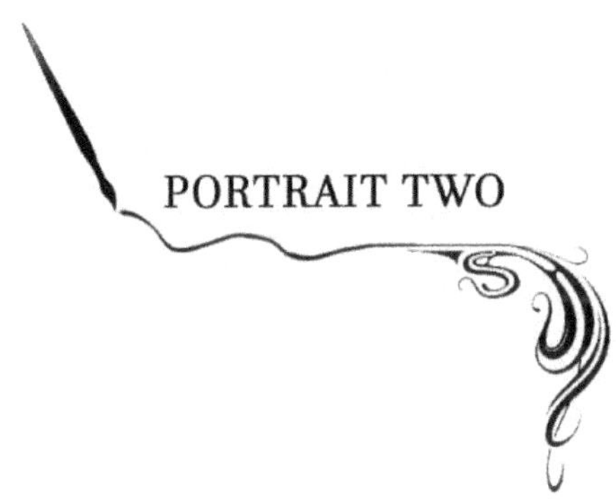

PORTRAIT TWO

THE METROPOLITAN MUSEUM OF ART

I worked my way through the evening with a rather detached modicum of enthusiasm as I set up the displays for the upcoming attraction. It was one of the cons to the job, if the art did nothing for me, certainly the job of putting up or taking it down had less than my rhapsodic spirit for the task. Egypt's latest tomb raid was now, come and gone, as were the rescued ivories that once adorned the now flooded temples of Zhongxiao County, China.

This week: Charles Buster's Hollywood Lost and Found.

Some things were meant to never be found once lost. That was an argument best saved to bore my imaginary date, while sharing after hour cocktails and thoughts of painting him after some brisk fucking. Not for the man who was assigned to assist me and certainly not to my employer.

Just because Renaud hired me fresh out of Julliard with a Masters so fresh the ink had yet to dry, didn't mean I had grounds to step out of line and insult the museum's upcoming guest or their prospective artwork. Such was the muse of art; one man's art was usually trash to most everyone else. But if it paid the bills or gave the artist pleasure, more power to them.

The real boon to my position here at the Metropolitan was I worked a few evenings a week and the rest of my time was my own. And I spent most of that working on my own artistic trash. To which it seemed of late, my Muse had forsaken me. Leaving me to dig through the mental rubbish, desperate to find some semblance of talent tossed out like a phone number I had no intentions of calling.

I stood before the finished display of the lion costume from The Wizard of Oz. The fur tanned hides used to make it were now stiff and coarse to the touch. And oh do please kill me— it shed little golden hairs over everything. Myself and my black slacks included.

Stitches around the shoulders hung loosely and largely overlooked by its current owner, as he was to believe such repairs cheated the costume of antiquity. It was hideous to look at. I didn't think any repairs, save for a torch, would have improved it any.

"They say they killed two lions to make the suit, when the actor refused to wear anything but authentic lion skin."

My young, naïve and flaming assistant, Dimitri, was always a galactic encyclopedia of worthless info. Nevertheless, now that I looked at the Hollywood relic with that oddment of trivia in my head, I was helpless to prevent the very imagery of that flatulent, fat fag wearing the lion skins like a trophy around the studio. The gluttonous pig probably even acted as if it had been *he* who had shot the poor African beasts, or perhaps he claimed the animals laid down their lives right at his feet so he could revel in their rich fur. The actor had obviously been dressed in the wrong hide. They should have just rolled him in bacon and thrown him to the flying monkeys.

"No wonder my Muse has abandoned me. Look at the rubbish I suffer to look attractive on display."

"There's a new bartender down at the Candy Club. And he is packing a pretty big muse. One look from you and I bet he'd jump into your pocket." Dimitri dropped his hands to his hips and rocked them back in forth to suggest I get my dick danced on.

"Hmmm, if he's that easy, chances are he's no muse for me."

My young padawan rolled his eyes at me with a heavy sigh, "Stop spoiling the pot before you've even tasted it." And he prissed off for our next corner arrangement, whether I had some snobby retort or not. "Besides, I didn't say he was a *muse* for you. Don't you ever just take them home to get laid?"

"Only in my head."

"Poor, poor, Johnson."

"Not so poor."

Dimitri stopped, shooting a glance over his shoulder at me with a spark of new amusement, "Oh? You keeping secrets from me now?"

"No," I chuckled, "Just semantics."

Another roll of his eyes and we headed down the hall. Dimitri had a certain pizazz for the swishy walk, like a *Lynx* strutting down the catwalk in the latest couture fashion show— minus the pricy couture that he could not afford— though I knew Dimitri would have looked spectacular in them, whether it be male or female or bizarre alien.

"I still can't believe you cut your hair," he changed the subject.

"Emerald Chromium Oxide green just wasn't my look." He volunteered the name of my most recent faux pas.

"You have black hair. Everything goes with black; besides, you also have paint thinners." Dimitri shot a disapproving over-the-shoulder glare back at me.

"It only works when the paint is still somewhat wet. Anyway, it will grow back. Better a trim than rip my scalp out."

"So, you cut your hair, but you don't shave?"

I reached up and smoothed down the tightly groomed black scruff that lined my chin and jaw line. It was really more a brownish black. A Black Oxide of Iron. "Never a chance of that. Beside it was only three inches off the sides. It's not like I buzzed it down to how you wear yours."

"Your ears are showing, I'm not used to it." He shrugged and continued on.

We strolled through the great room of Europe's finest kings, queens, and noble titles, knowing it would take us right by the front foyer and the security station. Dimitri paid his respects to Marie Antoinette.

"The queen who had it all." He bowed with a flaming wave of his hand, then kicked a foot out to add to the queer flair.

"Except her head," I abolished his idol worshiping.

Dimitri's shoulders slunk as he nearly glared at me, "You really are an ass sometimes."

I grinned, undoubtably proud of the title.

"So— are you going to come check out the new bartender or not? I hear he can suck a mean cock." He shot another flaring glance over his shoulder at me, "Which I am safe to assume even your mean ass could use some sucking."

The very insinuation put a solid smirk on my face. "Pun intended?"

"OH!" he yelped, though never lost a sway in his swish.

I had to confess, though, I would never tell him outright, but Dimitri certainly made the nights in the slumbering museum entertaining. Whether it was conversations or facetious banter, it was always amusing and never as dull as some of the displays we were commissioned to set up each week when the old went out and the new slid into its place.

About the only time Dimitri's neon-lit personality dimmed during work was when the security guards made their rounds and stopped to chat or watch. Tonight, the guys had a recorded game to keep them preoccupied and away from mine and Dimitri's duties. Some sport or another playing on a portable, so they weren't any more interested in ours than we were in theirs.

"Sports?" Dimitri had quirked up a brow at Ramone, who was routing his tablet into one of the security monitors behind the desk station, and a football game popped up just as we were passing through, "I say, what a rather robust group of fellows. Which color are we rooting for?" Dimitri tally hoed then actually sashayed off with an exaggerated strut with a hand on his hip.

Bert, who'd just returned with a fresh coffee, nearly spewed at the scene of Dimitri's sudden antics, then looked at me as if I were to blame.

"Don't look at me." I shrugged, "He's been hiding that goddess from you for some time."

"So— what gives?"

"I guess his inner *beeyotchay* wants out," I offered the queerest of explanations.

Ramone and Bert laughed so hard that one of them had to wipe a tear away.

Queen Marie, much like her head once did, fell away and Dimitri and I continued on until we arrived at the west second hall, where the statues of *Roúce Mallor* were to be packed for Newark.

The works of *Bisholamé* were coming in from Atlanta's High Museum of Art to take the spotlight for tomorrow's open viewing.

"Well?" Dimitri chimed at me and passed over the drill gun with it custom-fit bit for the crate.

"Well, what?" I ignored his intensions and carefully went to the task of unbolting the lids to each crate, already brought out by the museum's stock maintenance crew. Dimitri followed behind my movements and pulled the packing, stored within, for reuse on the art sculptures.

"You know perfectly damn well *what*. Why are you being so evasive?"

"You seem to think my sex life is your pet project." I stopped and dropped an elbow on one of the crates and took in a more thoughtful study of my compadre, watching as he tugged at the endless tangle of hay shavings and cardboard inserts. His eyes deflected away from any direct contact with mine. No wonder his Diva was out; she'd been crowded out of his small lithe frame, trying to hide something far more than just his inner diva. "There's someone else there, isn't there?" I said with more statement than question. "Someone who *you're* interested in."

The eyes started to roll but the execution didn't quite make it all the way through before his attention diverted elsewhere with an idle shrug, "I don't know what you're talking about."

"Humph— so why not just go and meet this *someone*? Why go through the trouble to pair me up with some droll piece of flesh?"

"He isn't droll— and— and, because."

"Ah, that clears it up." I went back to my crate opening. The *Because* game could take us a while and we only had so many hours in the night to assemble the displays.

"I'm just not like you," Dimitri finally said with a fresh layer of bashfulness. It was the very veil his inner diva hid behind on a regular basis. Why the flaming eye-batting queen winked his neon personality in my company was never discussed. But it was a selfdom charisma I was acutely aware was a private viewing and few— *very few*— got to see the truly brilliant and colorful Dimitri I had come to know over the past year, ever since he'd been re-assigned to tolerate my OCD idiosyncrasies. Hence, the reason we could never afford to dally on the job.

For the number of times we could normally go back and forth with the *Because* game, multiply each play by the number of infinite stars in our cosmos, and that's how many times I'll make Dimitri adjust the tilt on the newest Boudreaux being hung in the European gallery of painted art.

But oddly, Dimitri didn't add another *because.*

"Well, that was fast," I leaned in to whisper with a sultry vixen tease, "Are you sure you don't want to do a retake for, say, five or more *becauses* before spilling to me?" Then I sidled away to collect the first of twenty-three bronze statues of Gallic faery tales.

When Dimitri's retort didn't come in on cue, I quickly turned around to eye him skeptically. Dimitri was perfectly calculable, down to the last nuance even as the closeting veil fluttered up and down depending on the weather of audience.

"Have you ever seen the dancer Yanis Marshall?" his pop quiz completely out of context.

"Can't say I have." I shrugged and held the eighteen-inch Arthurian Morgana Pendragon in my hands as Dimitri stuffed protective pillows between her arms. We then wrapped her in cotton candy shavings, then followed with a sleeve of cardboard before I lowered her down in a bed of more shavings in the crate. "Ballet?"

Dimitri froze in a shocked glare then did a hip check with a fist, "You tripping?" he then turned to dutifully grab more packing for the next collectable.

I shrugged, my imagination going to the ballet theatre, and I envisioned my pole boy from Friday night bounding out from the curtains. In my mind's eye, he ran across the floor then leaped up into the air, catching his pole to swing around it several times, toes and leg pointing, arms popping with muscles. He went for the grand landing, tripped and the poor baby landed in my arms. Nice catch, Cavalier man, if I do say so myself.

"Are you going to listen?" the Diva called.

"Yes, Mistress Dimitri," I cooed, bringing the Pagan Priestess over next and finding a happy smile on Dimitri's face and a touch of pink to his otherwise Autumn Bronze skin color. Flattery always went well and far with my young padawan.

"Yanis is a choreographer."

"Then I approve."

"No. He lives in France."

"A dancer for a lover and a move to Paris. I most definitely approve. Why aren't you packed yet?

And oh perhaps, maybe you can find Queen Antoinette's wigs for your collection."

"I'm serious."

"My apologies."

"Ass."

I smirked. Did I say there was also no winning with him? What made you guess? You're getting why this is fun now, right? "Do continue then."

"He's such an incredible dancer and he always wears heels."

"Heels? Are we talking spikes or dog tricks?"

Dimitri scowled at me. "Platform heels." His hands worked on autopilot, wrapping the priestess in packing goods. "I love watching him in the videos. Delicious, spunky, and a diva queen." His hand floated to his heart and he feigned a tear of adoration, "It's like my inner goddess has escaped and manifested out in the world into Yanis Marshall and is having all the fun without me."

"Thus you want to be the Yanis Diva, then?"

"Pshh— no, of course not." He shrugged with a definite air of being defeated, "Yanis is already taken by Yanis himself. I want to be *Dimitri*! But I want to be the Dimitri Extraordinaire— who isn't afraid to wear his cat woman shoes where and whenever he feels like it. I want to be flamboyant on the outside, not walled up on the inside."

"So why don't you? Just be *you* and who cares about anyone else."

"Because I'm not like you."

"That's the second time you've said that. Are you saying only jackasses can wear pumps?"

Dimitri let out a laughing grin at that one. Why it was so amusing, I hadn't the faintest. Maybe he was trying to picture me stumbling around in a pair of towering foot killers. Such dreadful imagery should have had him writhing about on the floor in pain, not smiling, so I was back to not understanding.

"No. I mean *confident*."

"What makes you think I am confident?"

"Because you just walk right up and say, '*I want to paint you.*'" He put on his best deep-voice impersonation for the last bit.

"Don't mistake cocky for confidence. It's a ruse."

Dimitri gave me a flabbergasted look. "But the bois all follow you like lovesick pups."

"Lust-sick," I corrected and went for another statue.

"How so?"

"They think they're going to get laid. But that isn't the point of having them follow me."

"Then what is?"

"I have a muse to be fed."

Poor padawan. So troubled inside. A whole new slump arrived in his shoulders from the weight of yet another burdening reality coming down on him.

"My muse is turning anorexic because I don't know how to feed mine." Dimitri frowned. Such an unpleasant expression to live on his face. It had the likeness of a sad, purple puppy standing out in the rain.

I stopped and glanced at him. He really did need to learn how to get out of his own way and let that diva rule over his skin and bones. His inner Queen Sheba would know what to do. But I'm hardly the one to give advice on how. Again, not a clue. Like he said, I'm just an ass. And I only know how to teach Ass-elvish. "So, tell that diva bitch to step up and get busy. Then go out there and own it. Whatever it is inside you, own it, because no one else can. Take him for instance." I picked up the next statue to be packed away and held him up, "Do you think the Great Stag God, Cernunnos, can prance about the forest with an over grown rack of antlers on his head and sporting such a woody as this if he was afraid of what others might think?"

Dimitri muffled a laugh at the thirty-inch bronze figurine in my hands. The lower body something between human and Pan's cloven footed form though his well-endowed cock was still considerably human as too the rest of him from scrotum up, well, except for his extra, extra proportional size.

"It is pretty impressive. I doubt he could hide his six inch erection if he had wanted to."

"It's not hard to hide a six-inch dick," I commented ruefully.

"It is if you're only thirty inches tall."

"You are right, size proportionate. Let our lovers' asses be forever grateful human men are built as they are."

"My ass neither, though I hear that bartender is a power bottom."

"Don't praise power bottoms— they're pushy little bastards, impossible to keep fed, and I haven't time to keep one for a pet."

"Oh, and don't forget they tend to chew up muses," Dimitri added.

I stopped in mid bed laying of the endowed Stag god and glanced at Dimitri, certain the shock I felt was readable. "Is that what you did to Matteo?" Such scandal was not even acceptably tolerated behavior; it was better you screwed around than get jealous of an artist's muse.

Dimitri's lips twisted up in a tight pucker and he slowly, sheepishly turned away, "Uhmm— maybe."

"You most certainly deserved to get dumped left on the curb than."

PORTRAIT THREE

Ahh, the Monday-night Friday clubbers. That was us and there was a whole world of the likes for us to hang with at the Candy Club. My usual work nights with Dimitri were actually Tuesdays and Wednesdays with only the occasional variation, depending on the number of galleries being changed out or events that were coming up. However, Dimitri knew, that trying to get me into a crowded club during a weekend was hard pressed, so with the weekend crowd come and gone, Dimitri had managed to tow me out after all.

The bartender was everything Dimitri said he was. And everything *I* said he would be as well. Muscles from the gym, boy shorts that wrapped his glutei maximi cheeks like Christmas presents, begging to be opened. Not to mention his stocking was stuffed. He had too many bar patrons pawing on him for my liking, but his interests seeking wandering eyes seemed to becoming increasingly keen on me. Each round of drinks were a little stronger on the spirits and a little more swivel accentuated the body that delivered them.

"Don't you want to put the tip away for me?" Bartender toy asked, pressing his hips up within reach when I slapped the five dollars on the bar top. He swayed his hips, waving the waist band of his shorts to tempt me with a chance to cop a feel of smooth skin.

"No," I said flatly, picked up the new cocktail and turned my back to him to lean against the bar.

A sea of male bodies, each one looking just like the one behind me, only most with more clothes, undulated before me on the dancefloor. There were a few ladies in the mix, but they were always happy to be sandwiched in, in any way imagined or literal. It wasn't nearly as crowded as on the weekends, but still enough half-naked bodies gyrated and pranced about to lend it its name as the Candy Club. Just like any other gay night club. Name your cliché— it was probably out there on the dance floor. Gay— gay— gay— it was marvelous. And boring.

It turned out Dimitri had his eyes on Fynn Lei. *Seriously, where do these guys come up with these names?* I had to ask him three times to be certain I was hearing it right over the loud house music. Fynn leaned into me, pressing against my hand to let me feel his eagerness through his pants and his lips touched my ear as he recited his ideas of why I should invite him to my studio for painting lessons. Like I said, name your cliché. Now I had to add bad pickup lines to the foray.

"Sorry, I already have a line of waiting men." I turned, snatched the bill still sitting on the counter and waved the bartender over. I stuffed it down the front of his shorts and got a good handful of his cock in a sock. "Bar shift is over, fly boy," I said, turning to scooping Dimitri, along with the Mai Tai he was sipping on through a pink straw, under my arm and brushing him several steps away from the porn cheese king. I leaned in, my eyes on his. "Don't ever use me as bait to get them interested in you ever again. You'll only piss me off and your boy crushes will inevitably backfire. You have your own pros so learn to use them," I spoke just barely above the volume of music just as bartender boytoy came bouncing up, happy he'd bagged a winner. I delivered my last scathing glance at Dimitri before taking the toy out for a dry spin on the dance floor.

We hit the floor of bodies just as a dubstep version of *Deeper into you* spilled out over the sound system. The deep base caused the floor to vibrate with the beat and all I could think about was how repetitively cheesy the night had turned out. I had come out with a good mood, but porn and cheap fucks were no way to feed my Muse. But sock boy's body wasn't so bad once he had his arms wrapped around me like I was a prize. I allowed it as he made for good cover that I was rather lousy at dancing. He never even noticed, as his own swaying hips seemed to take care of all the necessary friction with good effect and, no doubt, well intentions. Even his hands were at work as they roamed over my arms and chest to feel me out. Once they were satisfied the artsy nerd here didn't rank too low on the musculature build, his hands took up home base on my ass.

"So— Dimi says you're a classic painter."

"Does he now?" Not bothering to be all impressed that boy-toy might show some interest. It was still small talk and he would either bore me with his tales of trying to be an artist or ask just far too many questions. But just then, boy-toy surprised me and threw me a curve ball.

"That's cool, my sister works at Fusion Event Planners. They do a lot of the fundraiser events at the Metro. That's where you work, isn't it? With Dimi?"

The music slowed down to signal the end of the night, and still boy-toy kept my hips in the right rocking beat with his and the drifting music. His hands still firmly planted on my ass, while mine mapped out curves and lines of his shoulders and arms, picturing them as they were transferred onto a large scale canvas in a melee of color and brush strokes. *Would I paint or break out the charcoals for this one?*

"I don't know the first thing about art, but they hold some great parties," Boy toy carried on.

I, however, was fixated on the predominant contours of the sternal head that created the sexy throaty dip between the clavicle bones. I even forcibly pivoted his chin around to display the corded tendon and sternocleidomastoid on the side of his neck for my scrutiny. Mmmm, it was quite nice. Not the most robust but would do well enough.

My Muse wasn't interested in sock puppets. Only lines and profiles of physique. How shadows and highlight played on corded muscle and popping tendons. And boy toy's were tasty enough that I would tolerate a bit of heavy petting just to convince him to come home with me. Turned out *convincing* wasn't required.

We caught a cab and turned away from Noho, going right past Soho, the village, and then turned left onto the cobble pavers of Broome Street, last to be dropped off at the corner of Chrystie Street on the outskirts of Little Italy.

I merely nodded to the two Italian blokes loitering outside the loading dock of the half-block-long warehouse, smoking cigars the size of their thumbs. They paid no never mind to me at all as I strolled by with a casual gait and my-*cough*-date in tow.

Waiting at the end of the warehouse, just past the narrow roll-up door, was a small set of steps that led up to the concave doorway. Three locks did the trick and I was holding it open to play the partial gentleman, "It's Josh, right?" Glancing over my shoulder, the man was just gawking at the building, his eyes running from one end to the other.

"Huh?" He finally looked at me.

"It's this way." I motioned my head through the door and up the steps to the top floor.

"Place is kinda shady. You don't worry about getting ripped off?"

"You know who owns this building?" I asked with some amusement as we climbed the stairs.

"Nu-uh."

"Louis Fitonnio, Grandson to Al Fitonnio."

"Yeah? Who's that?"

"A New York cousin to Al Capone." *I made that part up.* "If anyone, stupid enough, knocks off one of the Fitonnio warehouses, he and the next six generations of family are going to live very short lives."

"Kinda harsh for petty theft, isn't it?"

"You don't want to know what they do if you kill one of them." *I just couldn't help myself.*

We'd finally made it to the top, which was nothing more than a large corridor with the metal door entry to the upstairs studio and an old freight elevator at the end.

I gave the large metal sliding door a hard tug and it rolled with loud squeaky metal grinding along its track and opened up to what was my home.

I couldn't wait to mix my paints, feeling a refreshing energy as I flipped a few light switches on the panel just inside, not bothering to illuminate the kitchen to my right or the living space to my left. My focus was on the art. First and foremost, I needed to either do a quick outline sketch or some photos to preserve the moment, then send *him* to go get his own breakfast so I would be free to paint those lines in peace and solidarity. Thus, it was the makeshift modeling studio toward the back, and my artsy corner office, set dead center of all other projects that took up the warehouse floor, that got lit up and ready.

I'd hardly made it to the table that had been built into a tempera box, already getting side tracked, before I was picking out several brushes and a can for my mineral spirits. I eyed over which colors I would be playing with or needed to mix. The colors at the table called to me in a way a garden of blossoms might call to its gardener. Some fifty wooden troughs sat atop the tempera table, each containing its own pigment powder. Then Josh's words reached my ears and had my garden browsing turning into a decaying brown aftermath of weeds in winter in a snap.

"Your family name is no small prize for the picking, either."

I froze. Those very words severed my Muse like a hot knife to a candle. I hadn't told him my last name. Not that it should have mattered to the body of flesh standing behind me. "What did you just say?" Even I felt the shifting cold chill my mood was quickly creating in the vast upper studio. But when I slowly turned, hands filled with brushes and accessories, expecting to meet his eyes, instead I was looking at the back of Josh's hair, a color shade somewhere between Scorched Brown and Graveyard Earth. His glances nearly spiraled around as he took a 360-degree tour of my place. When I did catch a glimpse of his expressions, it was not amazement on his face or the earlier shades of vivid lust— but sheer disappointment.

"I thought you were supposed to be rich or something."

I *had* heard right and something had the hairs on the back of my neck bristling, wishing I had a Louis Fitonnio in my lineage. "How is it you know my family?"

"They're like one of the favorite contributors to the Children's Hospital and the Society of Preservation of the Classic Arts, or something like that." Josh turned and was finally looking at me, "Aren't they?"

"Tell me how you know that." I tossed my mixture can, and the stir sticks, to the floor and stepped towards him. "What game is this?"

"Like I said, my sister works for the event company that does all the fundraisers. When I mentioned Dimi might be hooking me up with you, she was practically throwing sponsored wedding bands at me," he chuckled then, blind to the fact he was pissing me off. "Dude, I don't walk off a good job for just any piece of ass."

Josh distorted with a smile but my brain was boiling like a pressure kettle ready to explode—despite the ice water coursing in my veins.

He still didn't see it and carried on, "She said your family was pretty damn rich. Even showed me an article from the paper of them posing with the city mayor at some party. My sister was convinced you were, too." Josh looked around again and shook his head, clearly not convinced I was as wealthy as he'd been led to believe.

"Get out," I managed the order through gritted teeth.

"What?" he asked, swiveling around to gape at me.

I flung a stern finger towards the door, "I said, get out!"

I turned away and just stood there. Frozen. I refused to even look at him. But finally, he left. The sliding door made a clatter as it was heaved to roll closed as hard as the man could force it. Not quite the door slamming effect Josh had effectively hoped for or getting it closed all the way either. I didn't care. I just stood there, staring at my empty canvas, feeling betrayed by it rather than by the man who'd been hoping to sack a rich hookup.

I sucked in a frustrated breath and ran my fingers through the mop of hair on my head, then swiped across my chin with the backs of my fingers. All that fidgeting before I gave in, folded, and then tossed the handful of brushes and charcoals I still held in the one hand toward the canvas and stomped off. I made it as far as the drop-cloth covered sofa, dropped down on it, and stared up at the dark pipe lined ceiling.

I'm sure you've heard your share of celebrity horror stories about gold digger relationships. Well, every word of them was true, for this wasn't my first encounter with one of my own. But the anger and displeasure I got from each never dissipated. After several long moments of deep breaths, and raking my fingers through my hair over and over, I glanced around the 2600 square feet of space, taking it in to see what Josh had seen. Most of it was taken up with what I called my canvas forest. At present, it contained eight wall-sized canvases, secured to angle arm trusses. Each one stood at varied heights, but all were taller than a man. Each station had a table, most of them cluttered with cans and cups coated with the color of their latest tempera used for their assigned projects in the making. Two easels were set up, with framed matte sketch paper. One measured three and a half feet wide by four high. The other had a coupe extra foot in height. Both, on the ready for my charcoal works for whenever my Muse finally came to participate.

Every canvas precisely stationed with enough space between them to get my scissor-lift around. The last canvas, at the far end, stood a towering twelve feet high and eight feet wide. That one, I kept covered with a drop cloth. There wasn't a drop of paint on it yet, but I kept it covered to keep it clean. Savoring it for that one perfect muse.

Beyond it and out of sight were my paint mixer machines for when I needed to make large batches.

My studio went on— a never ending project of working media but nothing to sparkle and shine of diamonds or gold for a mining bottom.

Along the wall, opposite the street-facing windows, which looked out over park across the way, was my photoshoot studio of fifty percent grey paper and staged with a number of studio lightboxes. Beyond the photo shoot area, all along the wall until the very end, were all my paintings and framed drawings of varying heights and widths. Stacked together in groups, leaning against the wall like ghosts. Each group hidden away under a blanket or cloth, waiting to be remembered, and put on display.

It looked just as a painter's studio should look— bare brick walls, rafter ceilings complete with pipe grid. A hardwood floor long since faded and forever embedded with decades of dust and dripped paint. But it was perhaps the small living space area where I sat now that was the most disappointing and a dead giveaway that I was not the man I was assumed to be. *Yes, yes, the ass part is me, but the rest is all a fool on you.* My sofa, for example, had lumps pressing into my back and shoulders, now reminding me, as it had for a year— or was it two?— that it was time to get a replacement. I ignored it before and just got one of those throw-over covers. A cover now decorated with the not so fineries of second-hand painted handiwork. Maybe this time I'll go out and actually get a new sofa.

But then that would mean I would have to replace the matching un-overstuffed chair that had long since lost all its interior fluff. That wasn't my fault really. I was dating someone for a bit— *I know, it's hard to believe, but it's true, and this is where you should pity me*— for I made the obnoxiously naive mistake of telling him he could move in. I really thought I had matured enough to take the next step. Not the L word mind you. Let us not get carried away with this storytelling, just the C for *cohabiting* word. That and he had convinced me it was the only way I would learn how to love someone. Of course, if any of that absurd notion had been true, I would have inquired of any presences, such as— the dog. But no— I didn't discover that until after Troy showed up with a beast brought forth from the very dregs of all unearthly creatures. He called it a Caucasian Shepherd. I said it was the very thing the myths of Hades' hell hounds was based upon. This creature made *Cujo* look like a cute little Pomeranian.

Troy tried several times to convince me it was a gentle giant. I just kept pointing to my ever continually diminishing furniture.

Now, come to think about it, shuddering as I thought about that beast, the conclusion brought me to believe it was the dog's fault for why my sofa felt so out of sorts under me right now. I did, however, find some use for the dog when there had been a string of break-ins along Chrystie Street. Walking a monster that dwarfed compact cars while yelling, just before coming around the corner, *Run, I don't know if I can hold him back any longer!*— has a certain impact on the neighborhood. It may or may not have helped that I had taken some paint and painted the dog's muzzle to appear a touch snarlier rather than like an innocent teddy bear.

It was just wrong that this colossus of a demon would betray you with such overt cuteness.

But back to the chore of walking the beast. Oh, the looks on people's faces just seconds before they ran off screaming. I may owe some thanks to Stephen King. Cujo-Godzilla even won us free Chinese take-out during one of those pleasant summer evening walks.

However, when the doggy rendition of artwork to my furniture was over, the beast made the fatal mistake of sinking its teeth into one of my canvases. That's when the dog had to go— so did Troy. It was a jubilant parting and to celebrate, I bought another set of drop cloths.

While my lack of living room décor etiquette continued, the kitchen however was sufficient. It even contained pots and pans. The *real* Louis from downstairs had a cousin come in and build the whole kitchen in the back right corner of the studio, with plenty of cabinets and a corner island that partitioned it off from the rest of the otherwise wide-open floor plan. I didn't ask where they got the cherry wood cabinets. Some things are better left out of polite discussion, as well as how he got me the bargain bin deal on brand new, undented, stainless steel appliances.

I did appreciate the upgrade. So, the old saying about never looking a gift horse in the mouth was applied here. It was a good one to keep handy when working with Italians.

Beyond the kitchen was a small sectioned off space I called the guest room, though it could hardly be called a room. It only had three walls, but it at least had a bathroom, closet space, and bed.

This pretty much concluded my place. *Down here.* Up in the loft where my room was, was a whole other world.

The one Josh failed to sniff out.

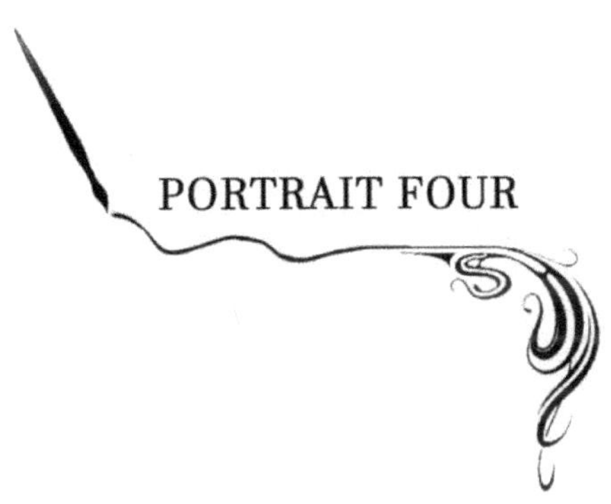

PORTRAIT FOUR

Two weeks had gone by and all I'd managed to accomplish was toss roughly three-gallons-worth of variously colored paints into the trash. Because night after night I stared at blank or unfinished canvases without ever having made a single brush stroke.

I rode up and down on the scissor lift with a spotlight, convinced that if I was looking from a different angle the new perspective would dislodge my thoughts, and I would see what the canvas wanted me to paint.

Sometimes I stared out the large plate glass windows, out towards the derelict park across the street or to the brick and mortar apartment buildings meant to blend in with the brownstones a few more blocks down, only to wish I had a view of the towering skyscrapers of Manhattan instead.

Still, nada— zilch— nothing— and it was pissing me off.

I finally decided it was high time I surfaced from my den of hibernation for something other than work.

I caught a cab like any good Yorky would and headed for the Candy Club, but when I saw the headache-inducing gold flashing marquee for the Pumping Station, I called my driver to a stop a good twenty blocks short of my original destination.

"Well, look who decided to drop by and let us know he still lives," David's familiar face greeted me at the door with a chuckle, getting in a good frisk and a shoulder rub before waving me in.

"You just like feeling me up." I grinned, feeling a peculiar air of sarcasm coming over me.

"You make my hand happy," he agreed to my accusation.

Inside the club was not as I left it last. Sure, it was stark and a touch on the swanky side. Low ceilings and dark recessed corners with dimly lit sconces set into the black ceiling pin boards, aimed straight down over misaligned tables. The bar took up the full right side of the club and the stage mirrored it in the back. But several of the tables were now fringed with white twisted swags of party favor crepe paper. And its own center piece of thick glass vases were arranged with white calla lilies and wrapped with white satin ribbons.

"What's with the new digs?" I asked Zane at the bar, who while without asking started mixing up a martini.

"Ha!" Zane laughed, "We had a bridal shower in here. They paid some big bucks to have the entire club dressed up."

I glanced around, seeing no bridal battle army and then back to him, "Glad I missed it." Zane nodded and shared a magnificent smile. *I was feeling better already.* "You know, you should come be my Muse one night," I invited.

He chuckled again, "Word has long since been out that you don't put out. Let me know when that changes and I'd be more than happy to pose for you as long as it includes your bed."

"You're killing me," I joked, but only partially. Was it really coming down to that? That I must pimp out my dick or my ass just to get someone to muse me? Such a sad— sad— sad— existence I must be that it has come to such terms. Not that I minded sex. Not in the least bit. I just often found it an inconvenience to whatever else I was doing at the time. It is truly a challenge to have sex and paint at the same time. The lines just never come out quite right.

I found a table, not too worse for wear after the white bridal invasion, against wall and sat down, anticipating to be entertained. A fairly muscular craft was on stage now, already down to his skivvies and sock puppet that bounced around gaily as he popped and gyrated his hips about to the beat of some older dance flavor. A few of the other male review dancers were out on the floor, either doing a table dance or hustling for one. One of them just happened to be my latest obsession— the suicidal pole vaulter.

He spotted me about the same time I spotted him and I had to scrub at my prickly chin to hide the virile smile I was apt to wear when he looked my way. Some visceral pleasure I had, like a lure of an intoxicating spell that reached out and tapped him on the shoulder and turned his gaze toward me. Then, with a flash of light, I saw within my daydreaming, the first of several test photographs before my eyes of just how I wanted him to pose. Which muscles I wanted accentuated. Adjustments made to the lights to angle down or up, catching the cords in his forearms. The planes of his abdomen suddenly rippling with hills and valleys not first visible. My mouth would water with need, my eyes would burn with desire. I wanted to taste him on my tongue, to feel him underneath me, to hear his moans of exquisite rapture. I'd move in closer to get another shot— planting a leg between his and leaning in to focus on the pulsing vein in his forearm. My thigh would graze his erection and he'd most likely hum. But when he dropped his head back with open invitation— it was the pose that did me in every time. I hardly snapped the last shot before abandoning the model to run for the canvas. Throwing off the sheet to one, driven to transfer the sight I'd just witnessed, captured in my head to the blank surface in a rough outline with charcoal pencils, before I would follow over the lines with the paints.

—etch —etch —circle— next, odd obscure shapes were spun from that one implement.

The world falling away, leaving me standing in space and with music playing in my ears to replicate my own movements and tempo. There was nothing else around me, floor and walls evaporated. No orbital passage— no night nor day. The stars could fall and dance around me, I never saw them. Angels could sing hymns of my coming death or the man of my dreams could be down on a knee to beg I propose to h—

I shook my head at the intrusion. No— no— and hell no— that would never happen. I have never told a man I loved him. For I loved only one. *My Muse.*

Suri swooped by in his snow-white latex boy shorts bringing another martini before I'd even finished the first. He liked the twenty-dollar tips he hardly had to bat a lash for, so it was a race against the other waiters to claim my table for that much at least.

I returned my gaze across the room to my pole dancer, now making small talk with the gent at the table. But when it looked like he was about to make his excuses, the large bear waved fresh new bills in my pole dancer's face to make sure he stayed.

I wiped my hand down my face and across the stubble of my chin, feeling the defeat. Ah but alas, he was much better off this way. I wasn't here to line his briefs with bills of invitation to sit on my lap. And I wasn't too terribly selfish to ignore that this *was* his place of work and those tableside dollars were how he paid his own bills. Why, I bet, he even had a happy sofa in his place.

On stage, the cops in a team of five gyrated around in syncopated rhythm, did their strip down number, and then tallied their dollars away. My boy-focus, on the floor, vanished off out-of-sight just as the sexy ride 'em cowboy tossed his Stetson over his head, and galloped about the stage for his performance, sending men up in a hoop, like cattle for the rutting before a round up. He even let one of the guys in the audience lasso him for a kiss at the curb of the stage.

Next up was space music coming across the sound system and moving mirrors bounced pin point light beams across a body recessed back in the darkness of the upstage shadows before flipping around to blind the audience. And then— *he* stepped forward.

His arms and legs were clad in tacky silver cuffs and shiny pieces. Silver metallic shorts fitted as if painted there. A silver yoke draped over his shoulders, falling in a V-pattern down his chest and matched the gaudy sparkly silver of his gauntlets. As more lighting was added to the spectacle, I could see someone had dusted his body with sparkles to add to the glitz, not too much but enough to invite the lightshow to dance over his skin.

It was a temptation hard to resist. Much to my amusement or to the gaudiness of his costume, even my tongue watered with the idea to romp and play. My fingers fell into a spell of movement, fingertips sliding in circles of each other as I watched for the flexing muscles to make their debut.

He took several steps, passing between the first two poles positioned at the back of the stage area, stepping slowly in tandem to the eerie space melody. A beat tapped into a climbing crescendo and female vocals cried out in one of those gooseflesh-creating notes, and my pole dancer took a dynamic step and leaped— his hands catching the center downstage pole just in time or it was going to be bowling night for the front row.

Arms went straight, locking into position, his body levitated over the heads of his audience in a frozen vault. And there they were, the stars of my show—

The biceps brachii, the triceps brachii, and the exterior carpi ulnaris— popping out in full glory. So miraculous— I amazed myself that I was not instantly chewing on my knuckles.

From that crescendo on, there was space walking up towards the ceiling as if he was strolling across the park until he pointed his toes straight up, parallel with the pole then snapped his legs down in a V over his head and shoulders, to either side of the pole. His body still pressed upward, defying gravity with the strength of one arm. Poses turned into fluid motion like a mixed cocktail of dance, gymnastics, and seduction. A mood flux of predator, prowess, and lover. Oh, how I was moved and captivated. And to such delights like that childhood memory as I watched Mikhail Baryshnikov flitting about the stage, I felt the thickening girth of my cock trapped in my briefs.

The music twined around the room with such moody vibrations that one could see colors in the air, sweeping back to the stage and joining the body in motion. Silver arms and leg pieces were flung aside as he spiraled into a more intricate serpentine of lifts, gambols, and helixes of limbs to match the antics of a mad man's mind ravaged with lust.

The finale was an astonishing pinwheel kick around an invisible pole then coming down to land in a crouching pose upstage and center. *Did I mention my hard-on?* Magnanimously installed.

The music grew faint. Then the performance was over, and the pole dancer receded behind one of the black stage curtains. But not entirely— a sliver of his side could still be seen as if on purpose. Just his right hand and the hip it hung beside. The veins that ran up his arms seemed to pulse with his very breath, begging for the eyes to trace it over. I shifted in my seat, thinking if I could get the vase, which obscured my view, out of the way, I might even catch a glimpse of soft flesh— and that's when I saw it.

I froze, staring at the vase on the table in front of me, then drew back just a fraction to refocus on what my eyes had seen. The straight line of the vase encased the glimpse of the pole dancer's body within its clear glass. And the curling petals of the lily that had dropped down inside the vase was near perfect to the shape of a pole dancer's hand.

Overhead, the white par-cans of light faded out and now only a wash of red, blue, and amber touched him, but I still saw that part of him. Only now he took on a whole new spectrum of illusion.

That was it!

I nearly sent my table, and the chairs around it, toppling over as I jumped up with excitement.

I rushed to the bar, pulled out a large bill and tossed it to Zane, "See he gets this and tell him I said *'thanks'*!" Then I rushed home as fast as I could convince my Lebanese taxi driver buddy to take me.

PORTRAIT FIVE

I spent two whole weeks making love to a canvas. Three canvases, to be exact. Brothers to each other, each containing a calla lily aligned just so, in muted stained colors. Laid over each of them was the grey silhouette outline of a male form that flowed perfectly with the curled petals of the flowers.

The greater change in the applied form of my art wasn't the subject; rather, it was who was wearing who. Until now, I drew their bodies masked with a flora of color as if they themselves had been painted and not the canvas. Now it was the color that wore the body. Every inch of the canvas was colored over and the physique of my subject snuck in like a grey mask. It was brilliant. And very much wet. But done.

I pulled a few paintings from the archive along the wall and scrutinized which of them, if any at all, would be included in my exhibit at the upcoming Summer Solstice fundraiser at the Metropolitan. It'd been five years since the last time I managed to gain a spot among the local artists, and I'd been praying and giving homage to a number of succulent gods and goddess before they departed the museum in their crates of swaddling in hopes they'd bless me and I'd not be turned down again for this year's event.

Only problem was— I was missing a centerpiece. Something beyond the others— the one that wowed the eyes and the senses within. The one that said *I am an artist to remember*. Without it, I would be a waste of precious space within the museum and might never get the chance to put my work on display there again.

I fetched my photo album and flipped through the endless pages of models, but before I even started I knew I wouldn't find what I needed among them. I tossed it down on the desk and let out a frustrated growl. We find objects of desire in the strangest of places. Mine just happened to be wrapped around a stage pole in a male review strip joint.

I performed a short ceremony of cleaning up and making myself presentable in a pair of jeans, an untucked white t-shirt and a black suit coat with the sleeves pushed up. Adding a touch of cologne, a light summer coastal fragrance by Tommy Bahama that went with every occasion, my favorite improperly matched ensemble was now complete. And then I was off for my destination.

When I arrived at the Pumping Station, I got my usual friendly pat down from David, then headed for the bar.

"Can I buy you a drink?" someone sitting a few barstools down asked, and I only assumed he might be asking me, since it was still early, and there were few others sitting at the bar. Each already settled down with a drink in hand. I locked my gaze with Zane, gave him a wink, and right away he was sliding a martini across the bar to me. Sometimes it paid to be predictable.

"No thanks," I answered as I turned away in search of a table, not even looking to see who had made the offer. Not really. I did catch some image refraction in my head, but I was more interested in the one I would soon see on the stage, and I knew not to invite small talk. Otherwise, next thing you knew they wanted to join you at a table and keep talking, and I wasn't here to talk or meet up. I was here to entertain my Muse.

I found a table along one of the divider walls. Not quite to the back as I liked, but it still had a good view of the stage, and I sat down on the bench seat that stretched out continually from one end to the other of the railed section that split the club into tiers.

On stage, a dancer was already stripped down to his jockey, working the five or so men sitting around the stage to get that one last dollar off them before his song ended. I sipped at my drink with little interest in the act on stage and enjoyed the anticipation that was building inside me. That is, until my uninvited guest grabbed a chair, flipped it around backwards, and dropped down in it, facing me instead of the stage.

"If you're waiting for me, you're facing the wrong direction," he said.

I was rather annoyed, but I did little more than open my mouth to say something before I clamped it shut again.

"Yeah, I get that a lot. The guys just don't recognize me in clothes."

I looked him over, clad in faded blue jeans and a floppy-fitting navy tank top. I couldn't argue with him there. I'd never seen him in street clothes before. In truth I'd never seen him up-close either and now I realized he was the one at the bar who'd offered to buy me a drink. "New act?"

He chuckled with a near boyish grin, but his eyes were half lit with lust. I had to wonder if mine often looked the same way when I looked at him. Even now with the clothes on, I liked what I saw.

"No. Day off. Just swung by to pick up my paycheck and schedule for next week."

"So— no performance tonight?"

"Nope. Guess it was lucky fate I was still here when you walked in."

"Lucky fate?"

"You came here to see me, right?"

I nodded, not bothering to argue if I was transparent or not. *He* was most certainly why I came. But without a stage performance it meant I was going to be leaving empty handed. And that was not acceptable. I was still in need of that peculiar stimulation, the one that sets the mind aside from all other thoughts of visuals, the one that saw the unexpected, captured the immaculate marvel, and then translated it into brush strokes. It was the stimulation that, as of late, only my suicidal pole-vaulting dancer had managed to ignite.

"Don't suppose there's a way to get you to dance on your day off then?"

"I rather like sitting here at your table instead." He was a smug, little shit, I could see, right from the start.

"How so?" I, in light of his attitude was keeping to my pragmatic ass-ism. One openly expressed surprise was all the stupor-reward I was going to give tonight.

"You always take off before I can get out on the floor. At least now I have you caught and can talk to you."

I almost laughed, but I managed to stop it before it got out, and revealed how nervous that bit of intelligence just made me.

I scratched at my lip with a finger, but I doubt it did anything to hide the heat I felt in my cheeks. My mouth felt dry and I bottomed the remains of my drink. But when I looked at my company's eyes, they gleamed all knowingly, like he hadn't missed a single nuance.

This was entirely not the planned evening I had in mind. Get in, get my fill, and get out. That was always the plan. Take my Muse with me and paint myself silly, well into the wee hours of the morning, for no man or master ever made great accomplishments by going to bed early.

But this one was breaking the rules on me suddenly. Now, I found myself floundering about without a contingency plan. That was never good.

My OCD was rioting and I found myself repositioning my empty martini glass several times. It wasn't that it was out of place that was the issue, it was that it was empty. Suri usually made a landing right about now with a second glass. Two was always my limit, then— Get Out. But there was no Suri and no second round coming. Just this tempter who was apparently calling the shots right now. "Can I buy *you* a drink?" There. I can do that, then Suri can take this one away and that would be resolved.

"I'm good."

I moved my glass and adjusted the napkin underneath it again.

"So, what's your name?" He scooted in a little closer, but remained relaxed while he watched me. Okay, small talk was good. Boring, but good. Names at least were good, pole dancer just seemed remiss of the phenomenon he was. But I needed to be relaxed as he was, so I sucked in a deep breath and relaxed back in my seat, then propped my arm up on the backrest. "Xherdan. And yours?"

"Sreven."

"Sreven." I rolled the name around in my head, "That's a very rare name."

"So is yours, I bet."

"Not if you're in Switzerland." I grinned.

"I tried tracing my name one time. All I found were three characters from fiction books," he laughed.

"It's Norwegian and very uncommon."

"Yeah?"

I nodded, "So, still no chance for a dance tonight?"

Sreven shook his head, "You need another plan."

I guess his good luck was still in the running, for there just happened to be an emergency backup plan I could fall on for this sort of roadblock. It hadn't been my plan A, but I wasn't about to go home without my Muse tonight. "I have an idea. Why don't you come over to my place and model for me?"

"Just like that, huh?"

"I can pay you."

"Sorry, but if you want a show, then you have to pay for them here. I'm a dancer, not an escort."

"That's good to know, except I just want you to model for me. Nothing else."

"I don't get it."

"I'm a painter." I could see by the look on his face he thought I was full of shit. I was fine with that, sort of. It was better than the false interest at least, but disappointing that it seemed he'd already been conditioned to never trust a guy for his word. I couldn't fault him for it, but I still didn't like being shrugged off like I was one of *them*. "Painting mostly, charcoal drawings on occasion."

"You any good?"

I nodded playfully and grinned. "I'm getting there."

Sreven sat there, still looking unsure of me, his mind probably shaking the book of knowledge overhead to see what clue slipped from its pages. *What was I all about? Was I playing him?*

I'd already said what I was about. But his mind wasn't too keen on accepting it at face value at the moment.

"You want to get a table dance?"

"No." I shook my head, but pulled out the bill I would have left behind for him before I left. Just like any other visit.

"If you change your mind—"

"No— wait. I didn't say *no* yet."

"You didn't say *yes* either."

"Because most offers want something. I'm not a rent boy."

"You've covered that."

"And you're okay with that?"

"I'm perfect with that." I grinned. It wasn't quite as fun as the *Because* game with Dimitri, but I was still amused by it.

"Okay, so where and when?"

"How 'bout now?"

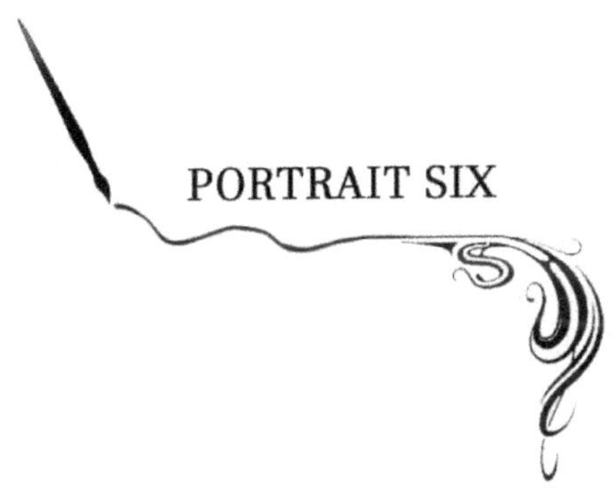

PORTRAIT SIX

"So— what do you want me to do?" Sreven asked as he glanced around, trying to make out the outline of the towering ghosts that loomed in the dark recesses of the warehouse while following right behind me so as not to get lost. After last time, I wasn't taking any chances with this one ruining my moment of having my Muse, so the only light switch I touched was the one for the back wall, just beyond the kitchen and spare room area, where my studio was.

I waved him over while I turned on the one lighting softbox, then the umbrella lamp, and then pointed him to the pile of neutral-toned cloth placed on the gray backdrop that also covered much of the floor. I grabbed my camera, fiddled with the settings a moment, then looked at him sitting cross-legged on the pile with his clothes still on. "Can you take your clothes off?"

"No," he said quickly and shook his head, "I'm not gonna have porn shots of me floating across the internet."

I almost grinned at that. Almost. Since I had never done such a thing. There was no such clause in the model release he'd just signed. And while there were a few rumors passed around about me, *porn operation* wasn't among them.

"How about down to your briefs then?"

He seemed reluctant, but for what reason I wasn't sure. He swung around that pole nearly every night in just his shorts. Why would it be any different here? At least here it was a step up from the Pumping Station.

Bending over, he tried to wrangle his jeans off, and I took advantage of this compromised position and snapped off a few photos. To test the lighting, of course.

He glanced up over his shoulder at me, with a not-so-thrilled expression, "Are you just after the undressing part?"

I clicked the viewer on the camera, brought up the image I'd just taken, then turned it around to show him. It was far more demonstrative than telling him.

"That's just my shoulder." He scowled at me.

"Actually, do you see the light shading that defines the active movement of your deltoid?"

"Seriously?" He still looked annoyed as if I were trying to trick him.

"Seriously," I answered and snapped off another, catching the definitions in his forearms as the jeans finally came off, and he tossed them aside. His tank top was next to come off and you can be sure I took advantage of the varying degrees in his back. Spectacular.

Stripped as far as he was going to, Sreven dropped back down to the pile in his black boxer briefs and waited for my instructions.

"Move around like you might be stretching or warming up into a routine pose." And he did, with not a single modicum of interest.

I dropped down on my stool, camera in lap, and just waited for him to stop wasting my time.

He looked like he was in the gym just swinging his arms, not giving a shit before sitting down to bench press a few measly dumbbells; not the dancer who was about to step out before the audience to deliver the performance of his life. I may have made a sniffling sound, perhaps even glanced at my watch, which was my way of saying I was bored, and losing my patience.

Sreven turned, glancing at me like I had just interrupted him, "I'm doing what you asked."

"No, you're not. You're trying to be a cocky son of bitch who asked for the job and now doesn't want to do it."

"What makes you think that?"

"It's written all over your body. I'm a professional observer of ass-ism."

"So, I'm just supposed to pose naked and not care what you do with the photos?"

Without a word, I twisted and grabbed one of the photo albums on the desk behind me, then passed it over to him, and then waited some more.

He flipped through the pages, turning each one in slow motion, his eyes scanning over one then the next. Bodies of physiques, some clothed, some not, but all were about the strength that showed in the pose. A guy who did martial arts caught in midair. An Army soldier doing push-ups while balanced on three wooden stools. A dancer standing on his toes with arms thrown back. A body builder bent over like Atlas straining under an invisible weight. A pair of beautiful manly legs whose hair was slicked down from water. Two arms bulging with corded muscles and veins that grasped a hidden head giving off a vibe of anguish or defeat.

"These are awesome. You should publish a book with them or something."

"That's not what they're for."

"What are they for?" He glanced at up at me for only a moment before returning to the mancandy within the album.

"To muse me only," I answered flatly, not expecting him to understand or care at this point. He didn't see what I saw. "They go in there until I transfer them to paint for those over there." I pointed to the forest of standing canvases.

He flipped several more pages, reaching the end. The last one in the book, a man in nothing but his maroon briefs was lowered down on one knee, and his right leg kicked out at his side, and he was bent back, propped on one hand, letting his head fall back and the dark black hair hung in a disheveled appearance. His physique little more than that of a swimmer's.

"Holy shit, who's that?" Sreven pointed to the last photo.

"Me. I agreed to pose in exchange for someone else's poses."

Sreven glanced back up at me then to the photo, "You cut your hair off."

"A hazard with paint sometimes." He definitely didn't see what I saw. He didn't see me for that matter. Nor for who I was. I'm never one to care what others think of me. Part of that ass-ism at work. Yet, here I was feeling it now, like a huge disappointment that life had somehow let me down. Again.

I placed the camera down and left Sreven, walked over to my forest of canvases and stopped at the smaller scaled easel with its sketchpad that was always out and ready for anything that came to mind. But nothing did. I just stood there looking at the blank white paper, with the black charcoal stick between my fingers. I felt the heavy sigh expel from my chest, but it gave me no relief. In a surge of frustration, I gouged out a giant X across it then dropped the charcoal stick.

I walked over to the table of tempera, but even when I circled around it, none of the colors called to me. I went to one of the large eight-foot canvas work stations, but the urge to pull its drop cover off didn't happen either. *You're done. Just call it a night, Xherdan.*

I turned, nearly colliding with Sreven.

"What do you want?" A redressed Sreven stood squared off against me, looking unsympathetically into my eyes.

"I want you to look me in the eyes and see only me— a painter— and not try to look for what everyone else wants me to be."

"What do you see when you look at me? Is it not the same as what everyone else sees? You come to the club like everyone else and you watch me spin around that pole half naked. Do you not desire me as nothing more than the hunky stripper boi? Isn't that why you asked me here?"

I took a step closer, my gaze falling heavily on the man before me, trailing over the contours that beckoned to be caressed and lavished, "I will show you what I see." I reached across the myriad of canisters, all cluttered on the table next to the huge canvas board, still kept covered from prying eyes, and dipped my fingers into one of the cans. I brought out a dollop full of Nickle Titanate Gold and rubbed it into both palms like lotion, then spoke softly to answer his question precisely, while my eyes never lifted from the muscles that captured me. "When you wrap your fingers around the pole—" I brought my hand under Sreven's arm and lifted it with a glancing brush from the backs of my fingers, "I see this muscle light up with a soft contour as it readies to go to work." And with that said, I dragged the palm of my hand over the long extensor digitorum muscle of Sreven's forearm, leaving it gilded in the metallic gold paint. I pushed on his elbow, bringing his arm out level at shoulder height, "And when you put the weight of your body into your grip, I see this muscle call me." Again, I elaborated my description with motion, painting another muscle with gold paint.

"When that amber-gold par can in the ceiling rafters lights up between the second magenta and cyan gels and it breaks the dark silhouette of your body—" I dropped my hand to his left shoulder and let gravity pull it down his chest, "I see this—" but at the last moment, I lifted my thumb to avoid painting his nipple. For that bit of his body, I wanted to save for my tongue.

It went like this for some time— more muscles to point out, when, and why— a new color of paint added, never losing track of how I loved and desired this body. And then I worked more colors over his flesh, filling in all the areas not yet touched by paint, "All that I see, suddenly becomes motion. Becomes fluid. The soul's expression. Your body is the art and it moves, begging me to translate it into poetry. But how can a man who is blindly in love with motion find words to describe it? So I try to use what I know— Brush strokes."

"But why do you leave when it's over? You never stay," Sreven asked, the very words practically gasped. As his breathing deepened with excitement and his eyes followed the path of my hands.

The very question asked was a plea, I heard the hurt in his voice, and I turned away to avoid meeting his eyes, "I can't bear the whistling and whore calls. It ruins the moment. So I steal away and bring the vision here where I can still enjoy some remnants of it." I glanced back only to have the pale mauve disc on his chest still carefully devoid of paint whispered for my attention and I couldn't resist another moment. When I dropped down to capture it in my mouth, I heard the excited hiss overhead and Sreven's arm wrapped possessively around my head to ensure I stayed right there.

It was a moment like this, when my visions of art transformed, and I saw us laid out over a nest of sheets, steam ghosting off our skin as we fucked in a chorus of grunts and groans. Damn—

I pulled away and stood. I should have apologized, but I didn't. What could I have possibly said? I'm a man with a dick.

"So you *do* desire me like the others?"

I winced or perhaps just blinked. I was unsure of what form of accusation it was, because he didn't sound pissed about it. "I'll call you a cab." I turned, looking over the table then the floor. Strange, I suddenly forgot what a phone even looked like.

A hand touched my shoulder and drew me around, and suddenly Sreven's mouth crashed over mine. I felt the very hand that gripped that brass pole cup the back of my neck while the other took my wrist and guided it around his waist. From there I couldn't be sure if even a poet could keep up with the fury of motion. Our tongues dueled not for control but just for more of each other, and hands grappled for more fleshy contact until we'd both realized there was too much clothing in the equation.

"Do you want me, Xherdan?"

"Yesssss." The very word took the full breath from my lungs and expressed just how much I *did* want him.

Passion ensued— it lit up like tanker fires put to match. We pushed, pulled and kicked off the majority of our clothes, and one of us fisted the drop cloth from the canvas board and pulled it down to the floor as we were to follow it. Few breaths were recaptured between breaks in our lip lock.

Sreven crawled on top of me, grinding over me in a feverish rocking motion that threatened to have me shooting off soon. I felt his erection straining to get free of his briefs and I had to oblige, forcing my hand between us and into his shorts, "Mmmm," I hummed. My fingers wrapped around his cock, loving the smooth silky feel of his skin against my palm. Kisses became breathy and sporadic as we glimpsed each other's expressions. I know most of what I saw made me grin madly, but the rest just had me craving him more.

Fuck, it felt good to have this body that I had watched for some time now moving over me. All those colors— I just couldn't let them go to waste, and I kicked off the floor, rolling us over until Sreven was laid across the drop cloth. I spread his thighs with mine and ground against him, my hand still working his cock. Sreven moaned and reached over his head, fisted into the canvas, and used it to anchor himself in the spiral of pleasure he'd ignited in me. The paints I had smothered over his skin transferred to the canvas in a pressed image of our frolicking. And then he let out a tight growl. His body convulsed with short jerks as he came in my hand.

When the racking movements subsided in him, Sreven was pulling me down for more kissing and more grinding. The cum that was splattered on my hand now added to the paint smudges on the canvas cloth.

"Tell me it's not over yet," Sreven pleaded against my lips, "I want to feel you inside me tonight."

Somehow, in all that, we were back on our feet, and we managed to cross the studio and up the stairs to my loft bedroom. Not entirely aware of our migration until I felt something hit the backs of my legs, and down we both went in a surprising *whoosh.*

The soft pillow top mattress, lost in a sea of downy comforters, caught me and then Sreven as he came down on top of me and relatively pinned me there. It hardly caused a disruption in our kissing and petting. About the only thing that did was the request mumbled against my lips as to where he could locate some lube and condoms. Then maybe the growl when he didn't like the answer I had. "In the privy."

Sreven sat up, and none too shy about grinding his tight ass against my trapped hard cock when he did so. "Why all the way in there?"

"I actually don't give in to compulsive sex regularly, so it's not located where you'd think."

With a defeated huff, Sreven crawled off me, and the bed, and padded off for the privy. I felt no true loss, knowing he'd be padding right back shortly. I simply enjoyed watching the gilded rainbow body in a whole new range of movements. The fine metallic essence of the paints captured the reflected lights of the city, and the moonlight from outside the windows, and made it its own, moving listlessly with Sreven's relaxed and more lackadaisical pace before vanishing into the bathroom. The light went on, the medicine cabinet opened, but then light— didn't go off as anticipated. I could hear a few more cabinet doors open and close. And there were quite a few to open. More than the average privy, I'd had it custom made with a full wall of cabinets, drawers, and alcoves so that whatever I needed was within easy grasp. A concept that was frustratingly lacking in most every home. I mean, who puts the linen and towel closet all the way down the hall at the far end from the bathroom? It only took one sopping trail of bathwater down the hardwood floors as a young teen in my parents' home and getting spotted naked and wet, by the housemaid, with little more than Mom's Mediterranean natural bath sponge to cover myself with, to know that *this* was a bad design of architecture.

The light finally turned off as it should have about eight minutes ago and the gilded rainbow demigod emerged.

"You're a very strange enigma. You don't even have aspirin in your medicine cabinet."

"If you have a headache, I have an all-natural South American tea downstairs that will take care of it."

Sreven shook his head with a disregarding shrug just as he was climbing back up on the bed, prowling through the jungle of comforters and throws, seeking his prey— lucky me. Then he bent down and kissed a lazy trail up my abdomen. I tucked an arm under my head, angling my line of sight, just mesmerized by his physique. However, inside, I already knew this was a done deal, and cabinet surfing was never a good trait. I had no opening for a lover who struggled with drugs. My attraction wasn't diminished because of it, but like a tasty food laced with cyanide, it was one of those things I just couldn't let in the door or put on my plate. "Were you hoping to score anything in particular?"

Sreven grinned, still playing kissy-kissy over my body, and once more shook his head, "No, just naturally curious. I'm sorry about it, but it's just a compulsive thing I have. You can learn a lot about people by what they have in their bathrooms. Especially their medicine cabinet."

"Like?" I was genuinely curious to hear his hypothesis of the insight to the human mind. Mine in particular.

"Like— if you have a lot of pills, you're either very sick, a hypochondriac, or got some habit problems. A lot of the guys I run into have the latter."

"What about you?"

"No way. Lost my best friend to drugs when we were still in middle school. I swore off them back then."

"So, what else can a medicine cabinet tell you?" I mentally granted him a second chance.

"If there's lots of band aids, then usually they're accident prone. Several boxes of condoms, they're players— those sorts of things."

Before I willed it there, a smirk had already established itself on my face, "And what have we learned about me this fine evening?"

"You're hiding something."

"How so?" His response surprised me.

"Because you have more luxuries in your bathroom than you do in the entire area of your downstairs studio. It's like a palace in there or something, and that's not including the attached walk-in closet I discovered." He paused to pull my free hand to his leg, encouraging me to cop a few feels while he talked, "You have two tower things with multiple jets in your shower and some giant square chrome plate hanging over the center of it. An entire wall of drawers and stuff. And I don't even know how to describe your sink and counter, except that maybe you stole it from a museum of modern art or something."

Have I mentioned that somewhere in all that sexy aphrodisiac body candy sitting on top of me, there is the ability to look completely boyish and naive? Probably not, because until now I had never seen it, but as his face scrunched up with the vexed thoughts over solving the puzzle of my life and character, it was absolutely adorable. But brief. It was gone when his hand produced the very item he had originally gone searching for. A single square foil containing the object required for our continued romp, should we ever get back on that ravishing ride.

"You only had one left in the box," he said it with a heavy amount of disappointment, waving it in his fingers, then dropped it on my stomach and just stared at it.

"So I'm a player?"

"I feared, but then I saw the date on the box." He looked directly at me then, his inner thoughts well-guarded.

What was he thinking? I wondered.

"The box is nearly eight months old."

"So— I'm not a player?" I teased him. I was liking this somehow. He had his little mini adventure in my privy— now I was having mine with his being stumped on the Xherdan Chantal Sudoku that made no sense. I didn't follow the usual formulas of human nature. I must have forgotten to keep my hand attentively working over him as he reached for my hand again that was resting rather idly on his thigh. He relocated my palm up around his chest, urging me to have my way with his flesh as he crawled over me.

He leaned down, "I don't know, but I want to find out," he spoke with a husky whisper, just moments before his lips found my neck.

Oh, the tide of sensations that washes over one's body with just the glancing connection of such kisses.

Did every man's spine melt and tingle down to his loins as mine did when someone kissed along his sensitive neck? Did I even care? No, of course not. For right now, I was completely self-absorbed. Save for one OCD moment. "You better have put everything back in its place after rummaging through my things."

There was a laugh between his attentive lips, "I may have left at least one thing out of place just to drive you crazy. Or to test how long it will take for you to realize what it is that's out of whack." Sinister little fuck he was. So cocky and proud suddenly. He ground into me, then pushed up on his elbows, bringing the foil up in his hand and tearing it open over my chest. All while still delivering minute kisses like drops of candy to my lips. The oddity of it was I got the impression, as one might do, that he was unfolding a napkin for his lap just before diving into a favorite meal. It was the seductive grin on his face that gave it away. But then the surging roll of his body, transforming me into his stage pole and visions of him dancing on the pole on the stage while I stood before him, filled the backs of my eyes and I moaned with escaped pleasure. *To hell with images of eating.*

"I like how you sound when you moan like that."

Then I felt his hands around my shaft and the condom sleeve rolling down. *I couldn't miss this.* I forced my eyes to open just as he rose up, his hand behind him, holding my cock in position, and then I felt the pucker of his ass, kiss the tip of my erection. Sreven eased up and down with small bouncing motions that lowered him by a fraction each time until I felt more of his body swallow up the glans of my cock.

I hissed, drawing my top lip between my teeth, and reached up, feeling over his chest and stomach, the moving art as he squirmed on top of me. He clearly was not wanting to take me in all the way at first, requiring some aclimating, but then I felt the breach of the first ring, and I sucked in a deep breath, letting out a heavy sigh that never stopped as he sank all the way down, taking me all the way inside his body. *To hell with acclimating. I suppose.*

"Oh fuuuck—" I hissed, pressing my head back into the bed, and rolled my hips up, going a little deeper inside those warm, delicate walls.

My hands found their own way to his thighs, clutching and caressing from one end to the other as I pushed my hips up to meet his gyrating pelvis. Already I found it hard to breathe. When was the last time I'd gotten laid? Months perhaps. My, how time slips past, but more importantly, when was the last time I had a dancer over my cock in such a sultry movement as Sreven did just now? Perhaps never. And Sreven was far more than just hips; his hands glided this way and that— over my chest, reaching for a shoulder, pulling himself over, hanging on while the rest of him bounced up and down to a desperate beat of the salacious symphony. A new tune in his head would engage and he shifted with the demands of a rhythm neither of us truly heard with our ears, but it still imbued us in some base form.

Sreven leaned back, my cock plunging ever deeper with every slide into his anal, and then I felt his hand between my thighs, catching my balls to massage them. He even friskily pushed a single digit beyond my tight sac, pressing over the perineum, and then tapping my own hole a few times. Insane bliss. For how else does one describe sex when in the deep throws of passion?

It's chaos— pure madness and pain when body and mind no longer coexist. Hands, cock, and lungs at war with each other, whether to stop or keep going, neither of any in treaty to do so at the same time. So, it was impossible for one to die of such stimulation, as some other part of the body was always still functioning, holding out to endure and seek out more pleasure just a little longer. So caught up in the storm, I was unware that my voice had joined the battle of expression.

"Fuck, the sounds you make turn me on." I heard the appraisal above me and his body rewarded me with a new sliding back and forth onto my cock, paired with the slapping of his own tumescence on my belly. "So fucking sexy," he continued. Only, while I was finally hearing the growling moans whispering some alien language of *yeses, that's it's,* and *so goods,* I was also aware that Sreven wasn't making such noises at all, and it hardly seemed fair that he was not.

It may have taken an age, but I convinced my right hand to give up its claim on a right bank of shore line on a smooth muscular leg and take up arms on Sreven's turgid cock.

"Ahh-hh sh-sh –shii— shit."

Ahhh, there was the sound I needed to hear. It filled me with a barbaric surge, some primal need that called the lines to press forward, despite the dreaded knowledge that in the final battle all would be shot forth and lost. But what was war without spillage, and how could a poet have recited tales of it, if the onslaught of release didn't come to blows as all battles should.

I tightened my grip and pumped over his cock in a steady rhythm, adding a bit of a twist to my wrist when my fingers engulfed the broad mushroom corona. And, oh— the cries ensued from him, driving me to keep going.

"Shii-stop. You're going to make me cum again, dammit!"

It wasn't quite the *beg-for-mercy* I was looking for yet. So, I ignored him. So did his own body, now gyrating, and then back to bouncing on top of me. My cock felt the very grip of his ass elevating our impending explosions. His hands now held out, fore and aft, to steady himself, for no matter what he said in words, his body was as determined as mine to fully engage the euphoria. "Stop. I'm gonna cum."

Again, I ignored such entertaining whimpers, keeping my hand in constant movement by pulling on his shaft, adding a glancing touch of my thumb over the weepy eye. I smeared the leaking clear ooze around those bundles of nerves that had even had madness seeming like a delight compared to the sensation that was now incomprehensible.

"Sh-shi–shit! Dammit, I don't want to cum yet. Stop!"

"So, stop," I mocked him.

He might have actually struggled with the command, given it a good showy try if the growl was any indication. But he utterly failed the simple task. His body remained in motion, rising and falling back down over my cock. "I can't. Fuck. I can't stop. You feel so go-ohhh—" and then it started. Sreven's body contorted, first thrown back in a breaking arch, then he curled forward in sheer pain as white ropes of cum shot out his shaft, over my hand, and onto my chest. Those power-hands of his latched onto me, anchoring himself lest he be thrown out into space with the surging explosion. *The victory was mine.* My head filled with the rancorous thrills of pillaging as Sreven folded over me into near collapse.

I wrapped him in my arms, locking on to keep from losing the position and the pillaging commenced. His ass was perfectly aligned, pitched up, for me to hammer into him with upward thrusts of my hips, and I gleefully did so in rapid succession. Not quite the pile driver movement and not the Energizer Bunny, but something in between. His ass cheeks slapped against my groin, making the fwap-fwap-fwap sound echo around the loft. I loved that sound, as well as the feeble moans that breathed against my neck and shoulder that showed he was too mindless to resist, and like any soldier, lost and wounded on the battlefield, he endured what pleasures I doled out as part of my concurrence.

I tightened my hold on him and kicked a heel into the bed, and soon I had us both rolling until he was under me so I could reposition. I pushed up on my knees, spread my legs wide to brace myself for better leverage, and I gripped his ankles, pushing them up high over his shoulders. I became a fucking machine. Sliding my cock all the way into his ass, switching in intervals of hard thrusts, and circular grinding.

This was when my laid-back-self vanished and the mostly-absent-domineering side reared up. Like a beast, I was up and in for the long fucking. Not giving up my own fire until I'd had his at least once or twice and, if possible, more times. After all, when one has lured a body such as Sreven's to his bed, one must deliver a fucking worthy for a demigod.

Sreven had a mind lapse where the only two words he knew how to say was *Oh fuck* and he said them often between moans and hisses. I liked them all with equal deviance.

It didn't take long before I felt his ass clamp down around my cock and that nearly ended my second wind right there. A minor retreat was all I could do to survive as I watched Sreven whimper. His head kicked back as hard as the mattress allowed. His teeth chattered and shivers raced over his skin. I felt his legs push against my palms and I allowed them to drop. I lowered down onto his chest and rode out the last of his orgasm with slow sinking pumps. Arms and legs wrapped around me. His heels locked at the small of my back and I didn't foresee any more hard movements for the rest of the night. Tricksy, little bottom had to have known that I was a doomed man with the slow fucking. Not that I figured I had much stamina left in me to go too much longer, and neither of us could breathe well enough to kiss, let alone another round of unabashed throttling. I felt the painful tightness in my balls with every slap of my groin against his ass, intensifying each switch from grind to roll against him.

I felt Sreven use his muscle control to try and rob me of mine. I actually growled and bit his jaw, curling my hips in to dig as deep as I could go.

"Shit, you're— an enigma."

But that was the last of my reserve, my will to hold out any longer spent when his ass juiced me for the prize, and I felt the bolt of lightning fire off from the back of my scrotum. It raced simultaneously up my spine and combusted in my thighs before drawing up tight into a ball of blind white electricity, which then fired out of my cock. Heavy growls, breaths, and moans came out in a mixed tenor chorus against Sreven's neck before I collapsed, utterly boneless, in his arms.

Sreven stretched out over me as we laid back, still tangled, silent, not knowing how much time had passed. Our hearts still pounding like beasts in our chests while our damp bodies cooled in the early, summer night air, with hardly an ounce of energy left enough to move a thumb in a caressing, post-coital connection.

"You're not like I expected," Sreven whispered against my shoulder.

Here it came, the proverbial meanderings of his mind, once more stumped at my cunning as I broke the rules of definition. I sucked in a deep relaxed breath, letting out a contented sigh to amuse him, and tucked my arm under my head while I still enjoyed caressing his side with my thumb from my other hand, "What were you expecting?"

"I don't know, just certainly not all this petting and cuddling stuff after sex."

"Want me to stop?" I raised a brow daringly to tease him that I just might. He snapped a hand up, catching me before I even had the chance to actually put thought to action, and he made sure my palm, and my thumb, remained in full contact.

"Don't even think of stopping. It feels too damn good. I like it for a change." He closed his eyes and let his head fall back to my shoulder, letting out a soft groan, and his hands welcomed the contact of my tracing. "I'm glad you're not who everyone says you are."

The chuckle got away from me, snapping him back into the now, "And what do they say?" Not that I was certain just who *they* were.

"Some of the guys at the club say you're an asshole, but I think that's just because you don't stick around after the shows much or buy table dances."

I chuckled again, letting the grin have its way with me, "They weren't wrong."

"What?"

"I am an asshole."

"No, you're not."

"Yeah— I am."

"Well, you're not like any asshole I've ever known." He folded over, then stretched his legs out to lay beside me, surrendering to the bed's calling with promises of deep sleep. "Most asses are aggressive, overly domineering, and they don't cuddle."

I turned my head and kissed him on the bridge of the nose. We do, when the right *someone* comes along, who feels comfortable for us, I thought silently. "I'm not your typical run-of-the-mill ass," I said instead.

PORTRAIT SEVEN

Morning came much too soon, and my guest lover looked far too precious, sound asleep in my bed, that I couldn't bring myself to wake him. Carefully, I slipped from his arms then vanished into the privy to shower and get ready for work.

I'd only been in the shower five minutes at most when I felt arms slipping around my waist, taking the soap from my hand to begin washing my chest. His lips pressed against the back of my shoulder and hummed against me. It was a nice touch even when I felt him playfully grind his growing cock against the cheeks of my ass. "You didn't wake me," he pouted from behind me.

"You looked too good as you were. Since you work nights, I figured you still needed a few more hours of sleep."

"You work nights too, I thought."

"Yes, but there's a staff meeting and they are in the day."

"You'd trust me enough to leave me in your studio alone, unsupervised?" He sounded surprised, a reaction at which I could only chuckle.

"I know where you work. Besides, if you're going to steal my wall size paintings, more power to you. As it is, the only thing down there worth pawning is the camera, and if you run away with that, you'll find yourself hard pressed for any invites to come back, since it's impossible for me to photograph you without it." I glanced over my shoulder at his flummoxed expression, which debated whether he should be offended or not, then he picked up on the sarcasm.

"I'll try to refrain myself, though it won't be easy."

His eyes shifted past me to the water features of the shower, seeing the 'thingies' in action. Both shower towers spilled water from a broad chrome plate like a waterfall, while the eight jets shot out pulsing spirals of water to deliver a pleasant massage. And the final display was how the large overhead square of metal that was now producing a rainfall of water droplets. "I could get used to this," he mumbled against my shoulder with a last kiss.

I twisted in his arms to face him, cupping his chin in my palm and drew him to my lips, his own just as soft and seductive as last night. *Mmmm, they were nice.* I nearly forgot my shower and the time as I nibbled on them until nibbling didn't seem to be enough, and with each connection, the yearning called and deepened the kiss until it had morphed into something far more demanding and greedy. And then I felt the ache in my cock, followed with regret of the reality kicking back in, forcing me to get moving and not in the direction I was presently. "Mmmm— damn, but I have to stop."

"There is always time for a quicky," he murmured, pressing back in, unleashing the greedy lover I was discovering lived in him.

"No." I asserted firmly, tore away from his mouth and dunked my head under the showerhead to rinse. My fingers splayed out and pressed against his chest to keep him from pushing back into me.

"They were right. You are an asshole," he huffed.

But then I felt Sreven's grip wrap around my cock and he gave me more than just a rough tug that had me growling and returning my attention to him. My own hand joining in momentarily. Oh, if only I could cum on his hand right that moment. Yesss— it would feel good to have a morning release before work. But I really didn't have that much time. I had already used up what small span of time I usually allowed myself lying next to him, just watching him sleep until I had no choice but to get up and rush out. Talk about making a terrible choice on how to spend my time, I nearly laughed aloud, then reached out and smacked Sreven's cock to reprimand him.

"I did confirm last night that I was." I grinned, leaning in to plant one final kiss to his scowling lips, then stepped from the shower, grabbed a towel on the way out, wrapped it around my hips, and disappeared into the walk-in closet to get dressed before Sreven could chase after me. Had he done so, he perhaps could've won the battle of wits the second time around. And I would have fucked him in the middle of my closet before reporting to duty. Oh, how the idea appealed to my senses— and my Muse.

As it was, I timed it just right, barely, and caught the bus when I sprinted up to Bowery. The whole ride, I entertained myself with visions of Sreven going back to my bed and sleeping the day away and, still being there when I got back from the meeting.

But it wasn't to be so.

The staff meeting was mostly reprising Dimitri and I that our next workweek would have four scheduled nights instead of the usual two with a repeat in the following next week, as several galleries needed to be changed out in time for the Summer Solstice Gala.

And while I came home to an empty warehouse to get a nap in before returning to the Metro and beginning those roll overs, I discovered one bit of good news. As I stared at the blank or half-finished canvases that would need to be completed right away, I found my masterpiece had already been finished. It was lying on the floor in a crumpled heap of off-white canvas, now rolled over and bearing the imprint of a rainbow gilded demi god who'd been ravished by an artist the night before.

Tonight, and for the next four nights, the grand gallery of the Metro would be draped off from the public eye. Going out was Assyria to Iberia at the Dawn of the Classical Age. Coming in was the Tour of Glass Art Chandeliers and Lamps, a collection of notoriety that included Libor Sostak, Petra Krausová, Petra Řehořová, and Michael Young. It also included a moving chandelier by Petra Krausová; a magnificent piece of work that, once hung from its robotic ceiling panels, would contain fourteen thousand individual pieces of blown glass. Each hung from an individual wire and programed to move up and down like kinetic rain to the slow fluid tempo of tranquil music so that, together, they mimicked flower petals floating on the rolling sea or the scales of a sea serpent's dance through the air in a routine that would take nearly two hours to complete before it started all over again. What a spectacular imagination had been at work behind such a mesmerizing creation. Especially to learn there was but only one other like it and it lived permanently inside the Singapore Changi airport and had been made by artist Jussi Angeleva.

It was a job detail Dimitri and I had no hand in once the Assyrian Art was packed up and carted away. Our job now was to sit there and not get in the way, which we figured we were quite well adapted to handle.

When the 'hands on' crew was gone, our time of lollygagging on the clock came to an end, and I could not have agreed more for the selection of floor exhibits that would be graced with such beauty hanging over them. For it was the Art and Architecture of Classical Greece waiting in their crates for Dimitri and I to unwrap, complete with a full-sized replica of Nike of Samothrace for the Grand Hall's centerpiece. The genuine Nike had remained a fixed resident of the Louvre in Paris, France since her discovery, and there she would forever remain. The only way to look upon Victory's headless winged beauty was to cross the ocean to see her. How beautiful she must be. Perhaps worth the trip so I could paint her.

Hmmm, perhaps. But for now, I was more focused on the man up in the bucket lift going from one hanging point, hidden inside the tiles to another, and dropping them down in preparation for the chandeliers. With long black hair pulled back in a ponytail, the muscles of his arms moved like a smooth machine as he pulled the rope up to him, and with it a chain that got clipped into a hook in the ceiling, then he'd maneuver over our heads in the lift to the next spot and do it all over again.

"I'm developing a fondness for the rigger's ass." I may have said out loud.

Dimitri glanced up and made googly eyes up at that ass, "Is that why you always call him in for the rigging?"

"I don't call him in. Blake is the one who handles the production calls."

"So, you're saying it's just coincidence that he comes in for the majority of them?"

I made a face over the idea, "I may have said we like working with him. He's very astute and careful around the displays." I shared a smug grin with Dimitri.

"Speaking of nice asses, I hear you had that pole dancer at your place last night," My prying padawan commented as we both sat back on one of the many benches that circled the grand hall. Both of us propped up on our hands with legs stretched out before us, looking all the part of worthless slackers that we could.

"How did you hear about that?"

He shrugged and glanced away. One could almost hear the innocent tune he was whistling in his head.

"Spill it."

"I'm not going to rat out my sources."

"I don't care about your sources, just what was said. Do these sources talk about your bed side manners?"

"I don't have any bed time manners to gossip about."

"Why not?"

Dimitri shrugged, "Because—"

Ah, we were on that now. Only I was certain he was using his *Because* game as a means to lead me away from the real question of the night. However, I was willing to play along for a bit. I never truly ever got sidetracked as much as Dimitri liked to think I did. "Because— why?"

"Just because."

"*Because* is a poor, slandering, informal, conjunction, adjective usage, being used as a forthright claim of cause and effect. Some form of action has led to you to respond in a particular manner— *be— cause—*"

"Because I have been giving some thought to what you said the other night, and—" he sucked in a deep breath, then let it out like a long heavy-hearted sigh.

"What is it, Dimitri?"

"I think I am going through a midlife crisis or something."

"HA!" I laughed and grabbed a full stem of grapes from his snack box. Ahh, the shy Dimitri was brought out in a pink haze that complemented his dark complexion. Dimitri truly was a doll to look upon at times, with long, black feathery lashes that would make most girls envious, and lips I gather most would love to ravish while their hands roamed over a body that was just this side of the androgynous fence line. But I also hadn't forgotten the last time he had used me to impress another in hopes of winning a beau of his own, and it looked like he had not learned his lesson yet. "Dimitri, don't make me get mean with you. What have you gone and done this time?"

"No," he snapped around, his face filled with worry. "I didn't do anything this time. That guy was a jerk and I'm sorry."

"They both were. So, tell me how it is you know about Sreven coming to my place."

"You know I've been going to those dancercise classes at the gym."

"This better be good, Dimitri," I warned him.

He flinched, either from the warning or he was recalling how the bartender boy toy he'd set me up with had seemed to have more insight into my life than I cared for strangers to know. Two incidences so close together and with too many mutuals was not going to weigh well on our friendship, and perhaps he was aware of that more than anything.

"Well, one of the girls in the class, Shelly, is always talking about her two male roomies. I had started to suspect that one of them might be your pole dancer because she's always talking about how one of them works at the Pumping Station and is giving her lessons. So, today in class, she mentioned he'd gotten an offer to model for some local painter." Dimitri tried not to grin, but it was a futile attempt. "I had such a hard time blocking the smile when she said that because I just might happen to know a certain painter who's been eyeballing a local pole dancer. What are the odds? So—" he shrugged then offered the rest of his grapes as a sacrifice. "It was him, right?"

I let out an easy sigh to show my relief. "It was him. Yes, I did have him at my place and you can keep your grapes."

"How's the painting coming along then? You did start painting last night, right?"

"In a rather unconventional sense of the word." I gave my padawan a wicked grin only to enjoy watching his jaw drop to the floor.

"You did not. You never—" he looked at me and I looked at him, just waiting. I may have given it away with a wink or something. And the sultry Diva was all in for the details. "So, tell me, how many times? Did he stay the whole night?"

The engine of the lift revved up and rigger-candy began his descent, "Oh look." I put on my best wicked grin, "It's time for us to go back to work." And I got up and headed across the floor.

"You're an ass!"

I love my life.

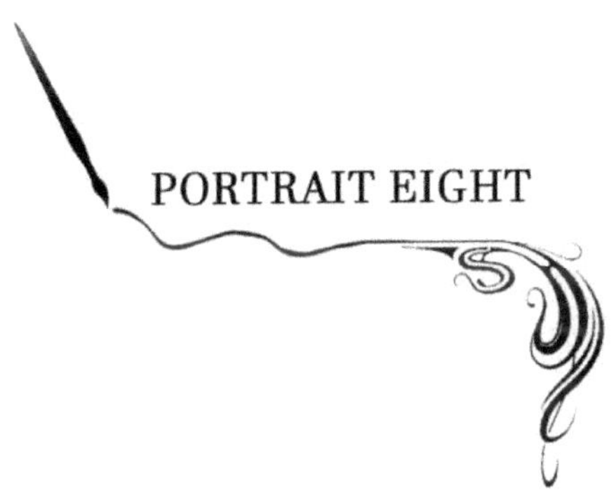

PORTRAIT EIGHT

The colors flowed through me and the languid rhythm from the music that filled the studio matched my movements as I swept my brushes over the canvas. My eyes always seeing far beyond what was yet there, but scrying the very transformation of what it was about to become. And all the while Sreven's physique moved around inside my colors, manipulating them into a swirling pool of liquid ecstasy. His presence not just feeding my muse, but becoming the very embodiment of it.

Golden ochre— Cerulean blue hue— Cadmium green— Chromium oxide green— Cool white—

Cobalt teal— Dioxazine purple— Indian Copper red— Indian Throne blue— chromatic black—

I took a step back, scanning my eyes over the painting in its current state of semi-completion. Fingers coated in an array of colors absently scratched at my chest, leaving traces of their presence there, along with the number of other self-inflicted deposits with far less purpose or designing scheme as what I'd created so far on the canvas. Every color accentuated a muscle form of the body I placed within it— trapezius— latissimus dorsi— posterior deltoid— needed more chrysocolla, a second cousin to Vermillion copper. Then perhaps a touch of folium, a deeper violet color to move towards the triceps group and the brachialis. And, of course, when I reached for it, it was empty. That's what I get for making small batches. But months of sitting up here, watching my paints dry, rather than dance across the white stage to the note of a dwindling supply, had motivated me to mix in smaller batches lately.

I took one last pause to absorb what I'd done so far, while once more absently scratching some part of my body, then tapping my lips with ideas and oh yeah, probably left some color there too. It was a constant haphazard byproduct of my workings that a good majority of second hand paint made it to my body and hair, making showering a joy when having to scrub all of it off afterwards. But for now, it was what it was. If I itch, I scratch. This constant renewal of byproduct also led to me wearing very little in the way of clothing while I painted. Less chance of ruining my clothes, and my body was far easier to clean. That which now brings me to share with you what I *do* actually wear.

For starters, I do wear something. It took only once having to try and get the paint off my dick to rid me of that skin freedom. But I did enjoy loose baggy comfort, so a pair of lounge pajama pants and a button-down cardigan was about it. Of course, there were no such rituals that it had to be a certain sweater or a certain color of PJs, as both would be tossed into the boiler furnace, once having succumbed to too much paint splatter to be comfortable any longer, and then replaced with the next set of garbs.

Alas there was no getting around it, I definitely needed more of that particular violet shade and the green copper, so I climbed down, snatched the cups and headed over to the tempera table. That's when my unexpected guest arrived.

The clatter of the roll doors going from right to left gave their arrival away. Admittedly it startled me, but then my eyes befell the Adonis body walking in that I recalled having slept with, and I pulled a small stereo remote from my sweater pocket and muted the music. "My Muse pays me a visit. To what fate do I owe such hedonism?" Whether he understood my regal quip was uncertain, but it did put a grin on his face.

"You know you're going to get robbed one of these days."

"Are you here to rob me then?" I chuckled, while I measured out several scoops of the chrysocolla powder into my cup.

"I may have come to steal a fuck or two." He raised his eye brows in a sultry mischievousness as he made his way to join me at the table.

"Ah, then you may be out of luck, for I have no fucks to give. I'm an asshole remember?"

Then a hand devoid of paint reached up, cupped my jawline, and pulled me around to face him, "Then, perhaps, I will have to give you a few of my own fucks, so you are never without." He started to lean in but his eyes dropped, they widened, seeing something he liked perhaps, and he leaned back to say as much, "Jeezus, you look sexy in paint." His hand dropped to my chest and my eyes followed it.

I was more than just dabbed in it, I discovered. Nearly my entire abdomen was streaked in a cascade of rainbow colors. But, I must say, it looked even better with his particular hand upon it. And it felt incredibly more so when it dropped down into my pants for a cheap grope. The kiss chaser was an added bonus. Tasting more of Gatorade or some similar sport drink was a nice change from the typical drunk kiss I was often offended by when being hit on. But my Muse wasn't done with me and my hands, despite all the thrill ride anticipation my cock was rising up for, began to stir in the paint mix. "I have to work," I mumbled against succulent lips bearing that salty tang.

"Mmmm, like work on me?"

"Very well," I answered agreeably and Sreven was quickly anointed in a finger-painted line of green copper paint.

"Hey!" He jumped back, his hand shielding the nipple I just accentuated. "Do you have any idea how long I spent in your shower last week, trying to get the paint off. No more!" He shot a scowling expression at me that was almost too tempting for me to not violate.

"Shame that. You might have looked rather well on stage sporting your own color array."

"Pass."

"Very well then. Move aside so I can paint on the canvas." I grabbed my cup of green and left him at the table.

"Asshole."

The title was sent after me as I climbed back up the scaffolding with my paint, until I realized that I'd forgotten my violet and had to climb right back down.

"But seriously, you could get robbed."

It took me a minute to catch on, then realized Sreven had picked up back where the conversation started before it escalated to painting his body, "How so?"

"The door gate downstairs was unlocked."

"Fire hazard."

"The studio door was unlocked." He wasn't giving up too easily, but I had it firsthand to know he was about out of fusses.

"Too lazy to come downstairs if someone knocks."

"And the steel door up here isn't very intimidating when it's just hanging on casters, and it wasn't locked either."

"So, what's your point?" I cocked a brow at him then began mixing my tincture.

"My point is, you live in Little Italy, Manhattan, New York— and you could get robbed!"

I stopped and looked up at him, "Do you know who owns this building?"

"Yeah, you told me that story, but most thieves don't give a shit who they are robbing."

"They do if they want to live." I carried my paint back to the scaffold and once more climbed up, much to the despondency of my guest, who was not thrilled at my lack of concern, "Look around you. There is nothing here to steal."

"There is always something to steal. And while we're on the topic, what's with the dog story?"

"What do you mean?"

"The other day— when I was leaving, some dude downstairs called out asking me if I locked the dog up. Told me I better have because the damn thing near killed somebody the other day."

"Yep. Almost did," I gave the nonchalant response while testing my new vat of color on the back of my wrist and compared it to what was on the canvas. Satisfied, I began to dab it into the previous strokes of color.

Sreven looked around and then I felt his eyes on my back, "There is no dog."

"Ahh, but the people down there don't know that." I reached back into my pocket, clicked the remote, and music spilled from eight large black boxes hanging from the rafters of the ceiling, filling every inch of air around me and my Muse with its intoxicating sound. I couldn't help to glance down and take one more look at him before surrendering to the images that would possess me. I'd done so just in time to catch a look, some expression that skirted around his eyes and made the muscles in his face twitch. What was it that had flitted through his mind when he looked up at me while music wrapped around him, I wondered. I need to pick up a book on facial muscles and map them down.

"I like this. Who is it?"

"Suduaya. This song is called Patience," I called down.

"You have their songs memorized?"

"No, just on auto play." I grinned then turned, taking my Muse's likeness with me and sent it to my hands. Keyboard notes danced like invisible fairies on my wrist. And I looked at my painting and became lost in it. You'd think I was high. That this mesmerizing event, as I became the puppet of both sound and color, was provoked by some unnatural source of influence. But I wasn't. Not in the sense of drugs or alcohol. Just the kind where magic made the human mind disembark, leaving logic and math behind. Some euphoric void that the artist withstood until color or image or some ethereal creation sprang forth and lit it all up. The very same materialization of an ancient magi's hand where black space became filled with a galaxy of stars. Sending scholars and storytellers alike to ask: why *is a raven like a writing desk?*

Thus, before me, the stretch of an arm materialized. A shading ran down, defining the tension along the bicep, then intercepted the tense rising of the brachioradialis. Yet, just as I was ready to bring the Cadmium gray down in a thin line to show the blood pulse, something out the corner of my eye grabbed me and ripped me away.

I froze at the sight of the taut form of a man kicking out a leg then holding it in a rigid ballonné, then he swung his foot back and twisting his body in a back outer-edge spin. Next a forward lunge, his arms thrown back in a stressed posture that made muscles and veins pop. I was spell bound.

Do you remember that night I watched my pole dancer commit backward bending suicide but jumped back from Heaven when I wanted to bring him home with me? Do you remember I said I didn't get a hard on? I'd be lying if I tried to tell you that this time, just like the boyhood moment when I had it hard for Mikhail, I was certainly establishing a bouncing tent of joy in my pajamas right about now. But it was far more than just my happy cock. My eyes— how they saw stars and my heart skittered gaily at the motion that bestowed upon me a private audience.

Sreven leaped and then kicked off into a double pinwheel kick, then launched again into a single aerial axle, to then return to earth to do some footwork. He flowed with a more modern contemporary fashion, with the emotion of tribal need, then a chain of toe turns, before dashing behind one of the canvas walls.

Just when I thought I couldn't take it any longer that he was gone from my sight, hands came around from hiding— then arms— then a strange twisting arc of movement; his arms were gone but Sreven's head appeared in a back bend, continued over into a back walkover, and landed on his feet. But what he did next made me weak in the knees. Up into the air he went straight up, his corded legs kicked up and to his sides in opposite directions to a full Russian aerial split. Not once, not twice— three times back to back. His feet came down at almost the exact same spot in which they started. A few more movements of footwork and then he made a final leap, landing at the last note of the song, bending all the way down over one leg until his forehead was touching the floor for his closing finish.

"Did you just do a Hopak?" I gasped in amazement.

His head popped up, remembering where he was, and he looked at me with surprise. "Yeah. You know what that is?"

I nodded.

"You know much else about dance?" He straightened and walked back over to where I was on the scaffolding.

"If I have seen Mikhail Baryshnikov do it, then it has a card in my Dewey Decimal System. Otherwise no, not really."

"Baryshnikov, huh?"

"First and only love of my life."

"I may have to try and change that." He grinned mischievously and scratched his nose. Too bad his fingers weren't tainted with paint as mine were; I would have loved to have seen the movement leave its imprint.

"Where did you go to school?" I was swift to change the subject, *just in case.*

"Here in New York. Mom, had a small studio for gymnastics and dance. I was really into the gymnastic part and got suckered into dance because they needed someone to throw the girls up in the air," he laughed and his super sexy whiter-than-white boyish smile grabbed me. "I learned from her and worked for her until she died. Now I try to afford weekend class sessions at Dance New Amsterdam when I can, just to keep learning and stay in training."

"I- I had no idea."

"Just a stripper, right?"

"No and yes. You have never moved like a stripper, but that's where I found you, too."

Sreven shrugged it off like it was no big deal. I just wasn't sure what part of that was being dismissed.

"It pays the bills where endless line-ups for try-outs does not." He glanced around, his attention going to the rafters, "Too bad you don't have any rope or silk cloths, then I could really give you a show."

I tucked back. "Who says I don't?"

His head snapped around to look at me. "Really?"

Within the next fifteen minutes I had a pile of rope on the floor with its looped ends tied and secured with a shackle to the scissor lift, and up we went.

The ceiling was already pre-rigged in several places with come-along motors that normally would be used for hoisting the large canvas frames up until I had their easels set in place— an installation compliments of a certain rigger I knew through work.

Each chain motor could hold a half ton, so neither Sreven nor his intentions would be a weight concern for them. Another ten minutes rigging it up and Sreven had a new toy to play with.

"No one's ever done this for me before."

I turned, finding him looking at me rather peculiarly. Like I had done something spectacular, but as to what I had no idea. Until he told me.

"Most guys I meet aren't interested in my dancing one bit. I don't know if it's too gay for them or just not a man thing. But they'd never look at me the way you did just a moment ago, or take the time to hang a rope from the ceiling for me to dance with. They see a stripper or maybe they see a fuck-boi, but nothing else."

I'm sure I was going to say something. I didn't know what. Could have been something totally suave and dashing, or could have just been my ass self. I didn't know. Neither will anyone else ever know what those words might have been if they hadn't lodged up in my throat, because right after the pile up, Sreven was coming over me in a deep kiss. Not as aggressive as he was the last time he took the initiative, but the dominant right hand behind my head still made it relevantly clear, I wasn't going anywhere.

Well, it turned out I was. *Down.* Sreven slowly started pulling me down to the board plank floor of the scissor lift, and he lowered over me, but all we did was kiss. Well that and some fondling. But for all my inability to ever grasp what goes on inside the mind of this hedonistic lover, the petting never grew heavy. No seduction attack. It was tender, almost like— no.

No, no, no, we are not going there.

But it was a nice suavity being kissed and held by my Muse.

You know that whole saying: *cuddling is great until one of you gets a hard-on?* Yeah, well, there's another one: cuddling and kissing is all good until the artist realizes his freshly mixed paints have probably already dried up in their cups. Realizing that, I forgot to contain the heavy sigh of discontent.

Sreven's head came up and he glanced down at me, trying to read my thoughts. Fat chance, and he soon realized that and had to ask for them, "What?"

"All that work and you still owe me a performance."

He grinned, rather happy for the demand, "I do, don't I?"

I nodded, then reached up and punched the button on the control box to take us down to the ground.

While Sreven got ready with the ropes, I strolled over to my raggedy sofa, and plopped down to watch. I pulled the remote from my sweater and flipped it to a fresh new song. I thought it was more energetic for a rope performance, yet it still had the exotic twang of a guitar sound pumping through a Lesley cabinet, accompanied with droning low tones coming from a keyboard.

Sreven took a moment, letting the music talk to him. His hands and feet seeming to take their place without a mental command. His wrist vanished inside coils of rope and he took a few steps, letting the reach of the ropes levitate his feet from the floor in casual lazy leaps. No true form or intention—

still getting a feel, and then his body seamlessly predicted the up-step in the music's tempo.

His arms tensed and heaved his weight up. His legs kicked up and over into a vertical vault. There was a pause, and then Sreven did an aerial split, after which he forced his body to tumble into the ropes to make them coil around his torso like a serpent. Another fanned-out kick of his legs and up he went, defying gravity by going up the ropes. He stopped just a few feet from the rigging in the rafters. He arched his back, letting his head fall back, his legs pointed out to create a horizon, and right on queue in another bridge of the music's rhythm, he came spiraling down. I jumped to the edge of the sofa, thinking *oh shit, I don't know if I have enough band-aids for a head-on crash with my floor.* Yet, Sreven came to an abrupted and calculated stop, floating just a few feet from what should have been his impending doom.

With only enough pause to accentuate the death defying fall, he changed it up and pulled an aerial a back walk over until his feet touched the floor and then he leaped off, sending his body into a front punch flip. After that, his movements, both powerful and smooth, were chained from one to the next. I could not keep up— not in words, because that was not my talent.

I leaned forward and reached under the sofa and pulled out a large pad of sketch paper and a box of various charcoals. My eyes fixated on the man caught in my ropes, watching the muscles in his arms go to work. I flipped to a clean sheet, selected a pencil and my hand did what words could never do. They created an imprint of Sreven's movements on the paper.

He was remarkable.

The music was now his lover and not me, and I was envious of such perfect matchmaking. One line turned into a hundred, haphazardly placed on the white pressed paper, but it soon began to take shape. My hedonic eidolon lover. My Muse in a physical form.

The song ended and his feet came to a stop, his chest heaving with thick breaths. He glanced over, but then the song started again and was instantly calling him to return to the dance.

"Does it ever end? The song?"

I shook my head, my hand still sweeping over the paper, adding more lines as I saw them in his body, "It's on a replay loop."

He grinned, then took off in a run and jumped. The ropes lifted him up in the air, and then together they twirled about out of control and into a whole new routine of fluid movement. And so did my hand.

I was sucked into a fool's paradise. Music enveloped us as he danced, his physique making love to my hand, moving it without conscious thought. He danced tirelessly for three more runs of the nine-minute song. How could this be taking place? He was too perfect for me to think he could be real. The song ended and this time Sreven abandoned the ropes and walked toward me. A look like the hunter closing in but not as a wolf over his prey, but the sheep demanding to be eaten by the wolf kind-of-gleam in his eyes and he wasn't leaving until he was speared.

His skin sheened with a heavy coat of sweat, his chest swelling with a heaving breath. My sketchpad forgotten, I let it slip from my hands just as he came down to straddle my lap and dove in to claim his kiss.

"I believe you owe me a fuck to give," he huskily whispered against my lips.

"Ah, but remember? I said I was all tapped out. In fact, I recall you mentioning something along the lines of you giving me a couple of your fucks just so I would have something to give," I reminded him.

"Mmmm, we'll work out some sort of credit line then."

Turned out I did have a fuck to give and I practiced using it as we made love right there on the sofa. The battered, lumpy thing is definitely going first thing in the morning.

After my line of credit was exhausted, we moved upstairs to the bed where we ruined yet another set of sheets while it was Sreven's turn to give a fuck. And it was a really good fuck that he gave me.

I lay in there, staring up at the canopy that draped over the bed, feeling sated and relaxed with Sreven more on me than beside me. Let me clarify, he was sprawled out across me. An arm and leg possessively pinning me down in more of that can't-get-away rather than the snuggle-up type of pinning. His head zonked out in dream world on my chest furthered his domain.

I kind of liked it. So much so that, the next morning, I remedied his break-in worries over my door with a key of his own to get in.

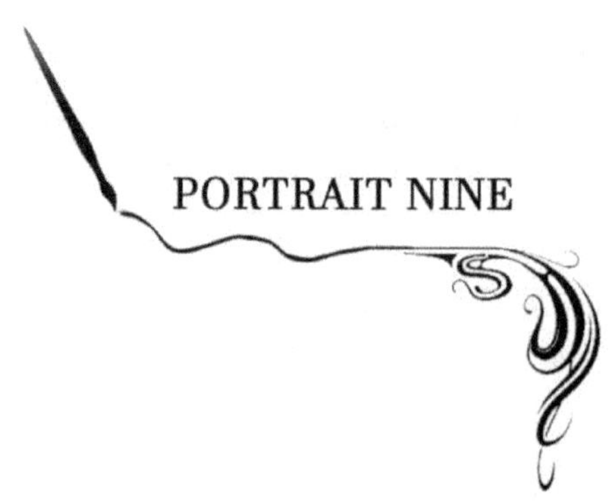

PORTRAIT NINE

The Metro was decked out in its full regality of flash-and-awe for tonight. For me, it meant another chance to present my works before the more prominent and wealthy— the mass of critics and collectors of art at its highest level of acceptance. A chance to stand among the classic displays, emanating as a product of self-discipline to improve upon the works of previous masters, demanding the highest standards of excellence and aspiring to the highest quality attainable. A chance to be separated from the Anne Elephants, Billy's cock sock paintings, and all the other modern impressionist of aesthetic relativism.

It had taken all five years, since working here at the Metropolitan, to get Renaud to overlook that I was an employee and that his selection of my work for the gala event was based on merit rather than biased in-house favoritism. Only, now that the day had finally come, I felt my cool—

Well, I have no earthly idea where I'd put it.

Like a pair of car keys, I didn't own, I still patted my back pockets and the lapel of my jacket as if my cool might be tucked away somewhere I could find, and could then slip it on like night shades.

I must have looked dreadfully pale before we left my place, for Sreven had made one final suggestion that I should don some eyewear. Having none of my own, we swung by his place to pick something up. He was very much the opposite of me— nighttime shades being a specialty of his it would seem. But we succeeded in narrowing the selection down to a pair of tea rose pink lens set in a pair of thinned-down, horn-rimmed frames. *A touch of geek to your suave*, he'd said to me before diving in for a deep rambunctious kiss.

The cab carried us the remainder of the way and dropped us off at the front of the museum. It was no small affair tonight at the Metro. It was the second largest fund-raiser of the year, with the Christmas party being the upmost top event where most sponsors needed to make that last contribution to count for the tax season. This was the Litha Summer Solstice Gala, held in honor of a time when the spring's seeding came into bloom, and so the pagan energy, usually about celebrating the Sun God, was put to good use for the museum, just like any good superstitious building would.

The event even came with a red carpet that draped down the front steps towards 5th Avenue and skylights, which swept around, to draw the city's night flockers in. Programmed Vari-lights moved and spun, changing colors and directions to wherever their programmer had them go, and illuminating the front of the sculpted architecture of the museum building with added flare.

To finish off the entry, there were two carved pyres lit to each side of the grand entrance. It was the spectacle of spectacles. And thankfully I was not the star of the show. I hardly doubted my ego could maintain the Hollywood pretentious act to pull off a grand entry such as artist Nigel Du' Vensuassi did. He was stopped just ahead of us, signing an autograph and then posing for a cluster of paparazzi. His all black attire with white silk tie and— oh look, someone told him to wear shades too. But his were a brash Cadmium yellow that drew more attention around his eyes rather than shaded them away.

I, however, in my warm rose view, slipped right by without notice. That bit of luck didn't last long however, for as soon as Linda Hampton, our curator of sales spotted me, I was being called over to the small kiosk desk station near the boutique to meet a special guest.

Special guest being a relevant phrase used respectively for anyone with enough money to buy originals.

"Xherdan, I would like for you to meet Mr. and Mrs. Fitzmaurice." Linda then turned to the man and woman, drawing their attention to me, "Mr. and Mrs. Fitzmaurice, this is the artist you inquired about, Xherdan Chantal."

"It's a pleasure to meet you, Xherdan." The man reached out to shake hands with me.

"Mr. Fitzmaurice."

"Please call me Nick, and this is my wife, Margo."

Margo was as lovely as any well-groomed wife could be, with a well-rehearsed smile that almost passed as genuine without coming across as insulting. Her brocade ivory colored evening gown held her in with a gentle persuasion, providing her with that ever elusive, though oft paid for, hourglass form, while cupping her bosom on a ruffled shelf. A sparkling shawl draped over her shoulders and crossed over her chest, adding some class to the otherwise exposed cleavage.

Nick was well dressed in his tux, like most of the men tonight, but he had a lighter less-than-snobby energy around him and his eyes stayed on his wife without ever wandering. And there was much to wander with. Gents and ladies in equal evening flair. Heels and bow ties. Perfume and red lipstick. Collectors, showers, artists, admirers, and critics. They were all here.

A teaming crew of servers endlessly crisscrossed in the crowd to hand out fresh glasses of champagne and hors d'oeuvres, while well-groomed hosts and hostesses directed and answered questions as the guests arrived.

Blown Glass Chandelier collections and the Nike of Samothrace effigy were in Gallery 899. The Modern Abstract paintings of Nigel Du' Vensuassi were upstairs in 206 next to the Chinese Buddhist Art, and the invited local artist exhibits were on display on the upstairs balcony, 202–204, around the lounge and bar. At least there, there was the chance that the more one drank, the better the art display would be received. Or one could only hope.

"I feel like I'm sweating," I whispered to my date.

"Mmmm, maybe later we can sneak behind one of those large statues and work on that sweating problem of yours," Sreven leaned close and whispered back into my ear.

I would have pulled up something equally lascivious to say, but we were still standing before the *special guests* and one of them was trying to talk to me.

"We just came down from the lounge and we saw your work. It's extraordinary. Very—" Mr. Fitzmaurice trailed off a moment, his tongue apparently looking for the politically correct word.

"Lecherous," I answered crudely. I just couldn't stand waiting for completed sentences with bated breath a moment longer. Bad enough I felt like my suit was sticking to my skin, but for words to get stuck as they toed about their path of approbation was just too much for me at the moment.

"I was thinking more along the line of *amorous*," he replaced my word with a jilted air of repugnant annoyance. I wasn't playing along and it showed. "We were hoping to either purchase or commission for a set of three?"

"All the exhibits are available for purchase. Linda usually covers that." I glanced around to see where the said Linda had vanished off to. This was clearly not my forte of affairs. Local newbie or not, it was uncalled for, for her to pawn her job onto me.

"Yes, we spoke to her about it, but we were more interested in the large pieces and she didn't have clearance on them."

"Oh." My head snapped around and I must have blinked like some dumb bloke for a moment.

I know— I was practically shaking my head at the slipped response. It was so unprofessional to let the socially adequate flaw slip and show my surprise. But I supposed it was bound to happen. I *am* an artist. Ever since I was a child, I have been an artist and have always identified myself as one long before I knew I was gay. However, being a painter in his spare time, and being one that makes money from selling his work, was a phase of existence all entirely separate. "That's very flattering, I think I can work something out. I haven't had much experience with commissioned pieces, so it would have to depend on what you're looking for." I really had no idea what to say, other than it would be nice to sell something along the wall-scaled paintings. "Perhaps you could tell me what your budget is."

"The budget isn't a problem. It's whether you can part with them. We have a private club opening up this summer, so we'd like to have them delivered in time for grand opening. If your work is about to go on tour, that may be a problem for you, which is why we are willing to pay for commissioned pieces for our club directly."

"I see. I—"

Then suddenly, Sreven was stepping up, "Why don't we go and take a look at the ones that have caught your eyes the most and you can tell us about your new club." He took liberties of them both, touching the couple with a hand to the back of an arm as he steered them for a stroll. "Then Xherdan can get with Linda after the event to discuss some options of arrangement that will have your walls adorned with just the right touch of eroticism. I have to say if you have Xherdan's work on your wish list, I am quite intrigued." Clearly, he was a natural at this flirtation praise game.

This gave me a chance to wave Linda back. First on the agenda was a scowl for throwing me to the wolves and then leaving, the next was to say *YES* but don't cheat me. In other words, I had no idea what the price tag should be. It wasn't a matter of me needing the money of course, but selling one's self cheap could kill one's career as an artist anyways. Just ask Annie the elephant. Some of her paintings had gone for a hundred and fifty grand. I'd like to walk away from this with a few more peanuts to boast about than Annie can.

Upstairs, along the longer stretch of wall space, my paintings and sketches hung. The Fitzmaurices babbled on about this line and that color. Sreven babbled right along with them as if it all had some meaning. Dimitri came to my rescue as well, bringing offerings of wine. "Thank you," I mouthed the words and nearly turned the fluke up all the way. It was dreadful, but wine nonetheless.

"Want another?"

"Yes, and thank you. Maybe find something stronger to drop in it while you're at it."

Dimity snickered. "I'll see what I can do."

"It was finally agreed for the Fitzmaurices to send an offer in a day or two," Sreven summed up the conversation's plan, just in case my catatonic mind had wandered off to escape and missed any of the important details. He straightened my tie then smoothed out my jacket as if my nerves might actually have wrinkled it. "But, for now, they've been sent on to enjoy the rest of the evening." It was Sreven's way of getting me off the hook of talking any further business on my night as guest local artist. It was nerve wracking enough already.

The departure with the Fitzmaurices went well, only to be greeted with another *special guest*. And then the moment came when Nigel was strolling through to see who had had the honors of gracing a wall while his masterpieces were on display in the larger gallery just a few rooms over and downstairs in the banquet hall for the event.

He spent nearly a half hour contemplating my centerpiece. Then another twenty or so musing over the one I called 'the dragon'. Three panels hung together. The center canvas was vertical while the outer two were hung on the horizontal.

Flashing broad arcs of Perylene red, Quinacridine magenta and Quinacridine red, gave way to talon-like movements in Transparent Earth red. Then shades of Terre Verde infused their presence so that at just the right angle, you saw the form of a body that had perhaps stumbled into the canvas, left his mark, and then fled before the dragon could coil around him.

"Who is the artist?" Nigel asked under his breath softly, leaning toward the two standing with him. Most likely one being his guide for the evening and the other his personal assistant.

I, for all my ass-ism and bravado, shrank away, hoping I became one with the wall behind me.

"Xherdan Chantal, a local artist chosen for tonight's local new coming artists."

Nigel nodded. The man actually nodded, then he held out a finger, wiggled it in the air. Not quite the symphony conductor— not quite— *no— it couldn't be— and yet—*

Eeny, meeny, miny, mo, and then Nigel pointed at my romping fuck-fest masterpiece. He paused, contemplated it, but then shook his head, going back to the dragon and then nodded to his personal assistant, who seemed to agree. Within a matter of minutes, Linda was catching up and she placed a white dot sticker in the lower left corner of the display card next to my painting, announcing that, as far as the museum was concerned, it was sold.

I let out a heavy sigh of get-me-the-fuck-out-of-here, watching as Nigel and his entourage sashayed away. "Dimitri?" My padawan was standing just a few feet away, his eyes bugging out, looking about as shocked as I felt. "I'm going to need that whole bottle now." He nodded agreeably and rushed off in search for one.

I felt a kiss press the base of my neck and I frolicked in it silently. It was a nice flip to the light switch for me and it took a good amount of the tension with it.

"I've just witnessed a whole new side of you in those last thirty or forty minutes. I liked him."

"Tell anyone and they'll never find your body," I half joked.

"Hmmm, can I put in a last request then?"

I turned my head to meet his gaze. Sreven's chin rested on the back of my shoulder while he looked up at me playfully, then wrapped his arms around me. "I suppose, I could consider one," I proffered.

"I want my final resting place to be stashed in your bed."

"I might be able to arrange that." I felt the smile coming up as he restored some semblance of my previous peacocking arrogance. As per customary reward for such services, I leaned in and planted a kiss on his nose to thank him for it.

Dimitri had finally arrived with a bottle in one hand and glasses in another. We shared a small mini celebration right there before the first sold painting to none other than Nigel Du' Vensuassi without having been robbed of my masterpiece.

I probably could have stood there and just basked in the memory of how it was made, given the one I made it with was wrapped around me, presently accounted for. But then a familiar body strolled by, and I knew at that very moment he was someone I wanted to talk to. My natural scheming shifted into high gear and a whole new plan was in the works.

"Say, was that?" Dimitri called out, pointing in the direction of the man I'd just spotted.

"Yes. Yes, it was." I grabbed Sreven and took off after the fleeting man.

Alan Wales was a local that had made his recognition for contemporary dance, and he had modeled for me on a few occasions. His upward jump that brought his feet in and he seemed to hover for long, frozen points in time were incredible. He'd also used my photos to his own advantage for his portfolio. Alan didn't owe me any favors, but I was hoping for a tune if I dropped a coin in the jukebox. A tune that Sreven could dance to.

It wasn't hard introducing them, and Sreven fell right into talking shop with another dancer. I, however, took a step back to spare myself the humility of looking the amateur of dance talk that would stain my reputation as a connoisseur from the theatre seats.

"If I asked you to tell me one dancer you hold as your closest role model, who would it be?" Alan asked. The charming smile he wore clarified it was for good merit of admirations, not criticizing.

"Gary Jetter, Alex Chu, and Josh Taylor. Maybe even throw Channing Tatum in there?"

Alan laughed then nodded, "That's a nice answer. I don't know who two of those were, but that tells me you're not picking names just to impress me. Tell you what, coming up in a few weeks there's this Annual International Contemporary Competition. I was registered for it, but I got picked up for a tour I couldn't refuse."

"Oh, I don't—"

"Trust me you do," Alan interrupted, "Don't ever give a shit about the *who* and *how* you get your invite or introduction. If it gets your foot in the door, use it, because you still have to do the dance. So, when someone says, '*I got a spot I can give you,*' you want to take it."

It was Sreven's turn to be flabbergasted. I kind of found that part funny. I'm not sure I could have ever pictured in my head, my bossy creature being at a loss of words. It was cute.

"You got something prepared?" Alan carried on, apparently not as swept off his feet by Sreven's newbie expressions of awe as I was.

"I've always got something laid out."

"Good, then be there, and don't be late." Alan pulled out his wallet, leafed through until he found what he was looking for, then handed a folded slip of paper over to Sreven, "This is the registry for my slot. When they say my name, just nod your head and show them what you got. Worry about your name later."

"I can't go in there thinking I have a shot at beating everyone out in the competition."

"Don't go there to dance for the judges. Dance for the scouts that are going to be there. There are troupes from all over the world that go to that competition." Alan reached over and tapped the paper in Sreven's hand, "They're all looking for the next dancer to add to the team, and that's not always the one who won the competition."

"Excuse me, Xherdan." Linda stepped up, wearing the expression that said she needed to steal me away again.

Alan made out the queue, turned to me, and gave me a pat on the shoulder, "It was good seeing you. Congratulations on the exhibit."

I started to step away to chase after Linda, but then recalled something and turned back to Alan, "Oh hey, one last question, please."

"Certainly." Alan paused, giving me one last audience with him.

"I saw a performance of you last year with a new dance partner. He wore heels."

"Juan-Juan."

"He is a he, right?"

Alan gave a laughing smile, "Depends on what kind of mood he's in. He can be a real drama queen at times, but he is a talented dancer. You should look him up. He lives here locally." Alan pulled out that magical wallet once more then handed over a card for a dance studio.

"Thank you." It may have been the first genuine smile I had put on for someone other than Sreven all night.

"You got some secret fetish for men in high heels? I'm not sure I approve." A playful tease, with a touch of jealousy, cordially whispering to me as we both watched Alan wander off.

"No. Just the shoes." And when I saw the vexed scowl from within my peripheral vision, my grin went back to its natural sarcastic state.

I spent the next hour bouncing between explaining why I did the colors and lines as I did on my paintings or recalling what weight of charcoal I liked in my pencils for my sketches. How my charcoal sketches looked almost life-like, even when compared to the black and white photographs I had included with their displays. How utterly scandalous the admirers felt, standing so close to the naked hedonists that stood life-size or greater on the wall, finding themselves wishing the images would come to life and step off the canvas and ravage their bodies. Between swooning admirers and shameless voyeurs, I shared the less drivel conversations with the man at my side.

Somewhere between all that, I discovered the *who's* and *what's* of the four dancers Sreven had mentioned to Alan. One was a famous contemporary ballet dancer. Another was this year's world champion pole dancer. I had no idea such a competition existed, though my jealous date made it clear he didn't want me to go investigating. I knew who Channing Tatum was. I know it may surprise you, but I have seen a few movies. Magic Mike and some step something or other being among them. Sreven's fourth selection had been an aerial silk dancer who'd done several tours with the infamous Cirque du Soleil.

I'm not a social butterfly. More the introvert type, but I am sure you've already guessed that much. So, for me, the vast majority of this night should have been a complete nightmare. It was just some fate of blind divinity that the cure was with me all along.

My advice to all introvert artists was this: date a stripper, or at least take one with you to all events. They will handle all the chit chat and small talk with a sexy smile. Their dancer bodies know precisely how to slip right against you and tuck themselves under your arm in varying levels of possession accordingly to each guest. It's extraordinary. How I wish I'd had one of these on my arm when my parents came to discover my artwork all those years ago. Oh, I would have paid to do that all over again. Then again— the night was still young. And I believed I wore that grin all night long after that. It must have looked indubitably hot on me, because while others were slipping out to the plaza or up to the rooftop garden veranda for cocktails and cigarettes, Sreven was dragging me into a utility closet.

A broom handle or something was jabbing me in the back in unbearable pain, but the body intent on seducing me wasn't about to give quarter for escaping. I felt the heat rise in the contact of his face, just from the intense scrubbing my bristled jaw caused, as we kissed like mad beasts. It was more a wrestling match with little resemblance of caressing. Sreven's hands were already shoved down my pants and had my scrotum and cock in one hand, cupping me with every movement, working me towards a full-blown erection that would in no way go down unless he had me cumming.

A tactic I had learned about Sreven was that he was a greedy lover, for certain, and he made sure his ass was the only cure for the level of horniness he pushed me to suffer. *Oh, it was a carnage of lust, no doubt.* A lover sacrificed to the gods who could now place great demands on me to be sated and to entertain the gods who created him. How had I been so blessed and cursed at the same time?

"God, do you know how hot and sexy you are?" Sreven started talking between kissing and nipping, "Watching you while people grovel or contemplate what wicked thought you might have entertained while painting is incredible." His hands released me to grab at my pants and shove them down beyond my hips and ass. My cock folded out like a dragon that'd just been freed from the lair. Sreven let out a growl and started kissing his way down my shirt until he found the long length of hard flesh that jutted out from under the contrasting crisp white shirt. "Then they all turn to you with lust-filled eyes, wishing you'd turn them into a canvas—"

What the fuck was he saying? I couldn't keep up when his tongue created its own brush strokes over my cock.

"Mmmm, *gah!*" I jack-knifed over him, my arms wrapping around his head and shoving him down until I felt my shaft hit the back of his throat, "Oh god, yessshhh." I fell victim to the moist suction, pumping up and down my cock. The hum he purred, added further vibration to a climbing pinpoint of electricity, gathering into a tight coil just to the back of my balls. *Oh fuck, his mouth felt so damn good.* His hands working around and over me like dance steps, moving about to catch one spot then another to make me crazy.

"Oh fuck, I think I'm going to cum if you don't stop," I gasped. I really do not know how I ever managed to hold a thought, let alone speak one, when he did this to me.

"The fuck you will."

I was suddenly popping free from the warm cosset of his mouth and he was moving back up my body, climbing me with a firm grip that I realized too late was meant to pull me down, and down we went in a loud crash, against what, I'm not sure. Nevertheless, I doubt there were any secrets between us and those out in the banquet hall any longer. The good thing was I felt something soft under me this time, instead of the broom stick.

Sreven was working his pants down from his ass and lowered down at my thighs already with condom in hand. He dropped the cap on my cock and passed the task over to me. He had the small pack of lube and was dabbing some on me while I rolled the condom down. Next, Sreven was reaching behind his back to prep his hole. It was going to be a full on assault, I knew.

"Hurry or someone is going to stop us."

"They can fucking watch then, because I need you inside me," Sreven husked with fever as he lowered himself. Just a few glancing kisses from his pucker, then he eased his way on without stopping.

"Oh *gohhd,*" I moaned exuberantly, throwing my head back. My hands gripped at his thighs in an instant.

I tried my best to contain my fervent enthusiasm as Sreven bounced over me, though it was a futile try with the silky walls of his hole clamping down to hug my cock with each landing. He dropped his weight completely, then ground down even further, rolling his hips back and forth, riding my cock in a wave of motion that was going to devoid me of that minute control I grasped to hang onto.

My hands gave little aid to such nonsense, as one held his thigh as it rode up and down with his body, and the other found purchase on a supply shelf behind me. That's when the racket rose up like a clatter, but neither of us cared. Just that climbing wave that carried us up high above the floor swept us about in a maelstrom of the unexplained. After all, I could never truly know what Sreven was feeling. If his body tingled as mine did. If, when he closed his eyes, his body went tumbling over like tumbleweeds in the wind. Did the ecstasy that pulsated out from his balls send tendrils of swirling sensation into his body so acute it could not be described? I could not possibly know these things, but one liked to think he did, as I did when I looked up at him.

Sreven's eyes rolled to the back of his head, his bottom lip completely ensnared by pearly white teeth. I saw the shudders chase each other up his torso and shiver out in his shoulders. Then he would growl and grind down even harder on my cock. I was sure every bit of it was made up in my head. Still, what I was seeing was hypnotic, and in one last breath my body heaved in violent shudders that forced me into a deathly contortion.

Sreven pulled his ass wide with one hand and shoved himself as far down as he could go, seating my erupting cock all the way in and pinching his muscles to close down tight.

"Fuck!" I cried out.

"Yesss." I heard him answer back.

I was floating in dark space, hardly aware of him moving.

"I wish I could have a painting of you when you're cumming."

Mmmm, damn. Was I supposed to have some witty response for that one? I hardly got my mouth open in my post bliss. I don't think I ever said a thing. Just reached up and grabbed his shirt and pulled him over for a kiss. Soft— pliant— well-fed— *content.*

And then came the knock.

My space voyage of euphoria was shattered, but Sreven's chuckle was a far better reaction than the one I was considering.

"Psst— you better get out here." I heard Dimitri's voice whispering anxiously from the other side, *"You're not going to believe who's here."*

Dimitri was no longer standing at the door when we stepped out. Sreven didn't bother tucking in his shirt, but he didn't mind giving me a hand with mine. I could see the blushed faces watching in my peripheral vision and it added some fun to it. Like a cherry placed on top of a sundae. "How about my tie?" I waved one of the hanging ends at him, but Sreven's attention was suddenly somewhere else. To something behind me. I gave it maybe half a second's thought. *You either look or just not give a fuck and walk off. Those were the options.*

I chose to turn.

Wow—

What can I say— but game on! "By Jove, there are gods watching over me after all," my response gleefully and instantaneously enamored. "I am truly blessed." And you can be sure the sarcasm dripped from every word as I spoke them. *Oh, don't get me wrong, I truly felt the gods favoring over me that moment.* However, the show I was about to put on was all for the couple standing just a few feet away, gaping with their chins on the floor and their eyes popping out from their eye sockets at me. Speechless as they were.

"Why— Mister— and *Missez*— Chantal."

I stretched out the emphasis of each word with definitive purpose. The ass was now behind the wheel and I went from happy-go-lucky-seduced lover to gloating pig in right about as much time as it took a Formula-1 car to make a pit stop. And the *gloatimus maxim-ass grin* I felt creeping up on my face could have powered all of Manhattan's energy needs for the rest of the night. "Fancy seeing you here. Why, it feels like it's been a decade since I last ran into you." I turned and looked at the beautiful man standing beside me with a fresh fucked glow to his face and a sated gleam in his eyes. This was just too damn perfect. And— I kissed him. I had to. To mark the moment of fate that only divine intervention could have put all the planets and stars aligned so that this moment could happen.

I loved the expression on Sreven's face even better when I pulled away. A lover that knew all was good between us. I felt no shame for us, nor would I pretend to. We may have just finished up fucking in the closet, but our lives were not closeted in any sense. And then I proudly turned to face my mother and father—

Face to face— offering them a condescending smile. The very same one I had just seen on Nigel's face while having to listen to the murmuring repose from an art dealer. "Have you enjoyed the art exhibits selected for this evening's gala so far?"

They couldn't even answer. *Poor saps.* Here they were, in their best evening attire, among associates and esteemed colleagues, to show off in a game of who could afford to give the most generously. To prattle on about this painting and that sculpture. And here I was, the son they most likely assumed vanished into a waste basket or gutter. Perhaps they had even forgotten I had ever been conceived. Their poor lost gay boy. Found— right dab in the middle of the very same Metropolitan Museum where they'd last seen him.

They looked— older to me. More than the ten years that had passed since the last time I stood beside them here. There was more to it, perhaps the effects of hatred eroding away their exterior beauty. As an artist, I understood the calamity such lack of pure passion affected the appearance of a person. The most well-groomed body held no attraction with a hateful dark soul, while the homeliest person could be radiantly beautiful because the peace within them glowed.

"What are you doing here? This is absurd," my father scoffed at me.

"Xherdan is one of the spotlighted artists for tonight's event." Possessive— bossy bottom— muse-a-licious— adventurous— and now I could add protective knight to the growing list of pros of this lover-of-mine as he spoke up with a surmounting hoity air of boasting pride.

"I must say—" I swept Sreven's hand in mine and brought it up in much the same way I had watched my father hold my mother's hand so many times. That *always* poised properness for the public. The hand in hand, then cupping them with his other hand. A connection my father always used to keep my mother's senseless babbling from running amuck. I even gave Sreven's hand a gentle pat to be sure my father noticed the pompously mimicked affection. "I was just telling my lover, *Sreven*, here," I added some emphasis to the Netherland name, "the night couldn't possibly get any better. But I see now, I was wrong."

"Excuse me," someone interrupted.

We all turned. Why, even my mother and father were finally able to move like mechanical humans do.

It was Linda.

"Xherdan, there's a special guest who wants to speak to you about one of your sketches." She shot a thumb over her shoulder, then excused herself to rejoin the client.

I turned to Sreven, who was stunned to say the least in his bewilderment, but I was the victorious villain who'd won the lottery of all vengeances. I grabbed him by the back of the neck and brought us crashing together. Enjoying the exaggerated crushing display of noses and lips against each other in a wet swanky kiss. "I will never doubt you again," I promised as I made eye contact. Whether he saw the wicked moment in my life or not, I didn't give one fuck about. I supplied him plenty of other tokens of fucks just for him, but this? This I gave none because it was all mine. But I was truly burning with a whole new lust to be given such a moment. *And to think— I hadn't even planned this one.* By god, it was staggeringly wondrous.

I glanced at my father, then my mother, and then turned as if they didn't exist, "Don't forget to leave your contribution at the gift table inside the banquet hall and do enjoy your evening."

And to make sure everyone else got a glimpse of my triumphant moment, I pulled Sreven against me and led him away at my side so I could strut and gloat on cloud nine, all the way up the stairs to return to the balcony where our love making painting hung.

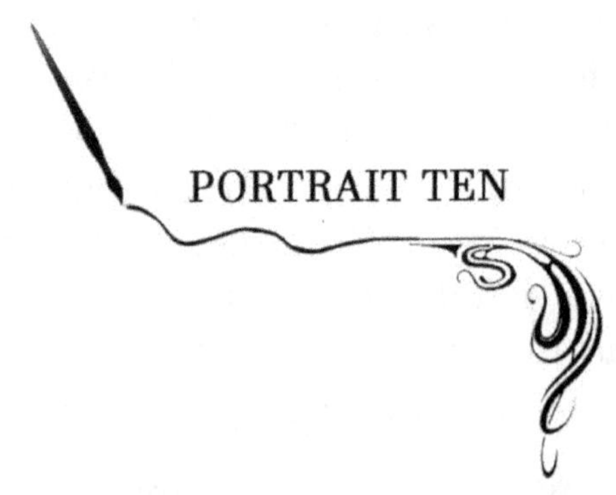

PORTRAIT TEN

"Can I help you?" a receptionist asked when I came in.

"Yes, I was hoping I could speak with a particular dancer here. Juan-Juan?" I inquired at the front desk of the dance hall where I was hoping to catch the high-heeled dancer I had spied Alan Wales dance with before.

"Sure, up the stairs and to the right. Studio hall 2-C."

"Thank you."

I followed the directions and stopped outside the door of 2-C and watched through the window. Four dancers were working out a routine while another dozen dancers were lined up along the wall watching. It stayed like that for another fifteen minutes and then they were all spilling out the door with gear bags in hand.

"Could someone point me to Juan-Juan, please?" I asked one of the young ladies as she passed by.

"Right over there in the leopard boots."

"Thanks." Leopard boots was certainly the best detail to point out, for the rest of Juan-Juan was not the diva one might expect. Like most of the other dancers, he was wearing a pair of black leggings, leg warmers, and a sloppy t-shirt with the sides cut out. It was just the average workout run-of-the-mill get-up. His long mousy brown hair was pulled up with a hair tie on the top of his head and allowed to flop over to one side. However, outside of the leopard-print high-heel ankle boots, it was perhaps the goatee that stood out the most. Juan-Juan, like myself, was a rule breaker, perhaps even better at it than I was, as Juan-Juan was breaking the gender rules of appearance. I liked him already.

"Excuse me, is your name Juan-Juan?"

He and two others turned and glanced at me. And I quickly did a shoe check to make sure I was in fact addressing the right dancer. "Are you Juan-Juan?"

"Yes," the goateed, high-heel dancer answered.

"My name is Xherdan Chantal. I'm an associate of Alan Wales. I was hoping I could have a moment of your time."

"You here for dance lessons?" He gave me the up and down, his expression denoting that *dancer material* was not registering on the Richter scale from me.

"Actually—" I couldn't help the laughing grin because I did love surprising people. "I'm here to ask you about your shoes."

PORTRAIT ELEVEN

This week's music mood was devoted to the works of Zack Hemsey. I was especially swept up by a tune called Vengeance. It was a potent driving pulse. Dark moody tones, a touch of angst, but not too brooding. Great stuff for painting to, and the words suited me well. Simple and to the point.

Before I die alone— Before my time has gone— There's just one thing I have to do—

Before the fire and stone— Before the world is gone— Have you some

> *patience— 'Cuz I will have my*
> *vengeance—*

> *Before I die alone— Let me have*
> *vengeance— Before my time has gone—*
> *I will— I will— I will have vengeance*

The damn song knew me and spoke to me. I'd had my vengeance now.

God, I loved my life.

Sreven came by a few times over the following weeks. He borrowed music to work with, and practiced in, and around, my forest of fresh new canvases.

I found myself often pausing in my work, the paints in the cups drying while I watched my hedonist jump and move around me.

Week two came to pass, only now Sreven practiced elsewhere. Finding *'a spot of floor with fewer obstacles'*, he'd said apologetically. I, however, still sat up top of my scissor lift, sitting on the open edge with my feet hanging over the side, arms resting on the handrail over my head and envisioning Sreven moving about the warehouse.

Even in his absence, he had the power to distract me.

Why, I even went out and bought a new sofa and chair. Then I invited Sreven to come over and christen them. He provided the wine and a brand-new box of condoms for the special occasion.

I, of course, was already mustarded and relished with paint when he arrived. Only, I wasn't about to ruin the upholstery of my new furnishings. So, I steer-horned my horny lover up to the shower first.

Sreven decided to have some fun with watercolors and commandeered the handheld while he had some fun of his own washing the myriad of rainbow splotches from my body. His fingers occasionally followed the wet streams of Armenian Bole iron ore red, Zinc White, Perinone Orange and Milori Blue. I must admit, those colors never touched me as finely as they did in that shower.

"Goddamn, I got lucky with you," he confessed his thoughts aloud.

He could have said damn near anything and it would have had the same effect on my body. The husky gasp with brain functions weren't exactly clicking logically. Sending exacerbated expressions to the tongue that sometimes came out gibberish as lust tried to be translated. And like I said, it wouldn't have mattered that I understood what he said or not. It was how it sounded, and the reverberating lust that emanated off his body— all that *Grrrrr* and *let me at him* mentality turning engine gears over inside the libido— made our cocks rise up and challenge each other in a duel of sword fighting.

And there was plenty of that once I stepped in to close in for a kiss. If that was what you wanted to call it; more like an inbred concoction of kissing, nibbling, and licking. Some chaotic, unpracticed intention to both touch all, and everything, at once, while at the same time trying to crawl inside the body I couldn't get enough of. It was anything but graceful or beautiful, narrated by the occasional gasp and growl with even the slightest glancing contact of cock on cock.

I felt the stubbly soft hairs of his buzz cut under the palms of my hands as I held his head, pulling him with an attempt to make him hold still for a deeper kiss. But there was seldom any success with that. Once Sreven got going, he stopped for no one or any reason. A ferocious appetite for sensation. And he knew every one of my weak spots.

His fingers raked into my hair and his lips closed in at my neck. The very first grazing connection, feeling his lips drag from the scoop of my neck, up to the spot behind my ear— chills raised up then back down my spine. When I felt teeth nip at the crook of my shoulder, I dropped my head back and could have easily just fallen back entirely if it weren't for the arms that coiled around me and held on.

Sensation.

Like colors, they shifted. Continually changing hue and pitch.

I grabbed the body shampoo and lathered some up in my hands then had some sensation play of my own. My hands slid over his skin with slick soapy caresses. He seemed thicker, his muscles more pronounced from the increase of practice and workouts. My tongue watered to trace each, but for now, my eyes were the ones being spoiled with the bedazzling view of Sreven's wet form.

Sreven, however, didn't agree and he soon had both mine and his cocks caught in his grip as he worked us up together. I found myself reaching behind him, teasing his hole with a wet finger to let me in. My finger found its way inside the silky soft walls. Sreven ripped from our kiss and let out a heavy gasp. I truly loved that sound. I don't know of a man who doesn't and I decided I wanted to hear a few more of those before we left the shower.

I turned him around and dropped to my knees behind him. Sreven had one of the most perfect asses, just the right meaty, growl worthy, bubbles of flesh, and I pushed the cheeks apart and moved in. Running my tongue from taint to tailbone.

"Ahhh, oh god," the groan was broadcasted over my head.

Torn between wanting to wear my victorious smirk and biting, I did both in a single act, leaving an imprint of my teeth in that perfect round flesh before returning to my intent. Water streamed down his spine and trickled over the puckered rosette. I lapped at the water and pink flesh, tonguing over the tender skin, then pushed in, burying my face between his ass cheeks. Every sound and shiver that came from Sreven urged me to continue. I reached between his legs, gently bent his cock back towards me until it was within reach, and I sucked the tip of his cock into my mouth. I swirled my tongue over it in the same mind-bending attack I used on his sphincter. I became relentless, conducting a symphony of Sreven-made whimpers and half-spoken words. Each nuance created a thrill in my own body. I dropped a hand to my cock and worked myself to near overload while I continued to use my tongue to work his hole. Goose bumps popped up all over his skin, and his hips pushed and pulled from my mouth until it was necessary to pin him in place so I could continue. Pushing my tongue inside him as far I could.

I slapped his hand away the moment I saw movement going for his cock, then pushed back up to my feet. I positioned my own shaft, so it was perfectly nestled between his ass cheeks, and then just started grinding into him. Sliding in wet skin. It felt too good and I found myself biting into the back of Sreven's shoulder, letting out a tight growl, but it was too late. The bone-rattling shudder ripped through me and my cock exploded over Sreven's back and between his ass cheeks. Even then, I found it difficult to stop, just enjoying the playground of warm jizz to slip and slide around in until the shower finally washed it all away.

Another shiver raced across my shoulders and I kissed the back of Sreven's head then whispered in his ear, "I want you to fuck me tonight."

He turned and landed into my kiss, his tongue pushing in to meet mine in a slow languid dance before breaking free to answer, "Your wish is my command."

I reached around him, turning off the shower and letting Sreven take over the steering. He walked me backwards out of the shower, then turned me to face the broad mirror, which hung over the sink counter. I watched his reflection as he pressed his lips into the back of my head and down along my neck. His arms wrapping around me, hands switching from gripping to cosseting, like dance moves.

He slid his cock against my backside, teasing himself with what was to come, until he reached across the counter, opened the medicine cabinet, and came to a complete stop. Intense blue eyes looked at me from our reflection.

"Where are the condoms?"

I nearly laughed. He seemed pissed, "Same place you left them the last time you gave a fuck."

He was not amused, "Which is?"

"Downstairs. Under the sofa."

His head dropped, slamming down on my shoulder and I heard a disgruntled growl come from behind me. *Poor soul.* But, alas, we were on the move again, padding naked and wet downstairs towards said misplaced box.

It wasn't often that we switched, but I did like the way Sreven topped. He wasn't the type to sit upright and drive inside me. Rather he wrapped around me, fully spooned regardless of what position we were in. He lay over my back, his arms wrapped around to grasp at my chest or feel down my thigh while he rocked his hips, circling and curling in, to grind his cock inside the tight confines of my ass. His lips never abandoned the attentive connection to my neck. Keeping me in a constant state of melted spinal cord syndrome. *Fuck, he felt good.* My head swimming within all that he was. Knees still firmly planted on the sofa, I pushed upright, using the back as leverage to press back against his cock. Enjoying every bit as much of the penetrating stretch as his thickened girth filled me. I could have tried to keep going to explain that it felt incredible, but you'd have missed out on all the small nuances and euphemisms of euphoria. In layman's terms, sex was purely indulgent with Sreven.

"Shi-i-i-t," he hissed in my ear.

"Yesss, exactly," I answered with my own husky breathing. Then reached behind me, catching his head and pulled him hard over so our mouth met in an aggressive crushing kiss. Hungry as we were when we were together.

Moonlight spilled through the large picture windows into the living space and over our bodies. The only music now was the steady hum of the city outside and the panting breaths we shared between gasps and groans.

A heated breath rasped in and out across my shoulder as he fought to hang on a little longer, his thick cock sliding in with as much sawing friction as his hands did over my chest. Drawing my insides to a similar intensity that was going to have me coming again soon. I needed his mouth for this, needed his kiss, and I pitched to my side, twisting so I could reach around, and grabbed his head, drawing him down. Our mouths became crushed together, yet unable to get a fixed lock. Sreven's groans deepened, signaling his release was coming, and his demands superseded mine, and I found myself getting shoved into the backrest of the sofa with Sreven thrusting his cock in deep, his movements turning carnal and wild until finally it all stopped. His face pressed against the back of my head and a loud grunt echoed in the studio. A hand reached around and gripped my cock, but he no sooner gave a couple of tugs and I was done for, shooting a rope of white cum onto the sofa cushions.

I collapsed under Sreven's dropping weight. And we hung there, over the back to capture our breath, before finally repositioning to stretch out over the sofa.

Somewhere in our drifting in and out of sleep, I was suddenly very awake with a strong urge to draw.

Snaking out from the coils of Sreven's arms and legs was always a challenge, but one I had managed with some practice, then pulled the pad of sketch paper out from under the sofa along with the box of charcoals that were always sitting on it. I dropped back against the chair and began.

I angled the paper some and laid out a few light lines to map out the lithe body that was sprawled out on my sofa. One arm tucked under his head, the other still wrapped around the ghost of myself. One leg bent, the other stretched out and rolled to just the right angle that the moonlight highlighted the sharp arch of his feet.

I must say I'd always had a thing for feet. But not just any feet. Most guys were flat footed and it was a bodily feature that often had me glancing away, but Sreven had phenomenally deep arches. Sexiest fucking thing I'd ever seen on a man's body.

I was almost finished when he stirred. Then that sleepy, contented face woke and searched the room, finding me over his shoulder. "There you are."

Neither of us moved. My hand froze over the paper, my eyes captured by his somnolent face. Not sure what emotions he was experiencing, but he finally broke the moment with a request, "It's cold here without you."

That was my cue and I slid the spiral pad back into its hiding spot and crawled back into my possessive spoon's arms.

"Xherdan?" Sreven whispered against the back of my head.

"Yes?"

"I've decided I'm not going to go to the tryouts."

The very suggestion sent a cold chill through me. An unacceptable one and I was soon rolling in my place so I could look at him, "Yes, you are."

"No. No, I can't. I'm not good enough for that kind of thing."

"Better to stay top man on the pole than take a chance to be the newbie on a different bigger ladder, right?"

He didn't answer. Which meant he knew precisely what I was talking about. "Do you have any idea how hard it was for me to get that spot at the Metro for the gala?"

"You work there, so I'm sure it just took some persuading."

"Try ten years of persuading and getting turned down before finally getting another shot at it. So, the last thing I was ever going to do was say my work isn't good enough to cut it to be among the likes of so many master artists."

"But I don't dance like the people who run this thing. I looked up the sponsors and the judges for the panel. Most of them are into classical ballet and some contemporary. Not a whole lot of modern."

"Good. So, don't dance like them. Dance like you want to dance. Show them what you do, not what you think they want to see. Blow them away, then walk out with your head held high." I got up from the sofa and headed up to the loft to my bed with Sreven in tow where the conversation continued.

After our long talk of precisely why Sreven was going to make sure he made it to the rehearsal tryouts, I'd enforced it with some more long hot sex. Even told him that if he didn't go, all this great stuff would be gone. For I just couldn't get myself involved with a non-dancing dancer. I'd meant it as a joke, but as we laid in bed in our post cooling cuddles, it'd apparently had a much different effect on Sreven's mind.

"You remember when you were talking to that guy, Alan, at the museum?"

"The one who gave you his spot for the tryouts? Yes, I faintly recall running into him," I answered sarcastically.

"He said something. When you asked about someone he'd danced with last year. He suggested you should look him up. What did he mean?"

"Alan? I don't know. He's modeled for me a few times. I guess he thought I might be interested in having his friend model for me as well."

"Why would he think that?"

"Because most people, who know me, know that pretty much the only thing I am ever interested in is having someone model for my Muse."

I wasn't entirely sure of the importance of that information, but I supposed it answered what curiosity or missing piece he had in his mind, for after that we fell silent and eventually fell sleep.

I was dreaming. Standing in a forest of painted trees, standing up like paper cut-outs. A fine mist, illuminated by glowing colors, blanketed the ground and rolled like a sea of spilled paints. Ahead, something moved about.

Elegant flowing movements, powerful motions that soon started to take on the shape of a man— slight movement closed in around me, bringing with it a draft of chill air, and then a bright light cut across the scenery like a spotlight that swept across the landscape and stung my eyes a moment before it faded— when it did, the figure that had teased me was gone.

I blinked several times, hoping the apparition would reappear, but instead I found myself looking up at the canopy over my bed and feeling the cool absence of a body that should have been lying next to me.

Something didn't feel right, but a glance in the direction of the privy said Sreven hadn't gotten up for a bathroom run. However, the minuscule glow of a moving light from below said something else. I just wasn't sure what. So, I decided to go find out.

I made my way down the railed stairs, seeing the moving light coming from under the back wall area below, and sure enough, that was where I found Sreven. Like a cat burglar, he was unveiling several of the stacks of canvas leaning against the wall, then leafed through them the way you would through a filing cabinet. I watched from the foot of the steps as he did this several times, until one in particular caught his interest, and he pulled it out to prop it against the wall. He took a step back, pondering it, then lowered down cross-legged before it and just stared at it. I had a good guess to what muse had been the source of that selected drawing. And I realized there were a couple of ways I could react to this, most of them shitty because it was a shitty feeling I got from it, that made the pit of my stomach twist up. I could pick from any one of them, and it would have been within the way I should have reacted, but then I never was any good at doing what others thought I should do.

I let him have his time there.

I didn't know what thoughts he had, but I gave them time to tumble around in his mind to either solidify or lose fire. Did he see what I saw when I looked at the drawing? Did he have any idea that he could draw my attention away from any one of those paintings, just by walking by? Did he sit there and try to see through my eyes? For, from my two-dimensional view point, he just sat there, not moving, his knees drawn up, and locked inside the hug of his arms. And for some crazy reason, I felt the urge to sit with him.

So, I did.

I sat beside him, legs crossed, knees drawn up like his. My arms wrapped around and locked with one hand holding my wrist and then leaned in until our shoulders touched.

"He must be an amazing dancer."

I shrugged, "He's more known for his jumps."

"What?"

I nodded to the sketch of Alan suspended in the air. Arms thrown out to his sides in relaxed display of finger grace. His legs drawn up, one out before him in a bent angle, the other tucked heel to ass. The shadow on the floor suggested he'd jumped so high his feet were where his head should have been, "I captured it rather well, actually."

"Did you love him?" The second question came just as flatly as the first. But it still took me by surprise. And that seemed to be happening a lot lately.

"We'd never even gone on a date." I shook my head.

He glanced at me, then back to the drawing, or rather to some speck of dust on the wall above it, "But you fucked him, right?"

"No. Alan is straight."

"If he had been gay?"

"No." Again, I shook my head. I'd had so many similar conversations with Dimitri, who always seemed to be surprised how infrequently I got laid, despite my thinking about it all the time. "He only came to model for me."

"You fucked me." He finally looked along his shoulder at me.

"Yeah, but you *didn't* model for me," I answered as I pushed myself back up to my feet.

Sreven was quickly twisting around to look at me, "Wait. Yes, I did mod—" he stopped mid word, seeing me as I directed my eyes to the small studio spot next to us, then I turned back to look at him. I grinned smugly, because I still wanted photos of Sreven, despite the plan change. *Which,* was another one of those outcomes I hadn't planned.

"Wait. Tell me. What are we?"

I stuffed my hands into the pockets of my sweater and drew in a long breath, then shrugged. "I don't know. But I like it."

"So, you just like me?"

"You make it sound like it's meaningless."

"It sounds meaningless the way you say it."

Touché.

"I don't even know what love means, Sreven. If that's what you're wanting to know. I love colors. I love lines and shadows. I love challenging myself to capture movement in my art. But people aren't the same as curves and lines and shades of blue."

"Have you ever loved someone?"

I didn't even need to think about that answer. There wasn't a moment in my life I had ever even contemplated the notion. And I was already shaking my head. The sad part was, now I had some idea maybe of what he'd been thinking about, but I wasn't going to say false words to comfort him. I'm just an ass who was, for the first time in my life, experiencing a soft spot for someone, or he simply impassioned me so completely in a way others hadn't. "Come back upstairs and finish the night with me. Don't go home with all that junk in your head." And I turned, because I wasn't sure he was actually going to come up.

This was new territory for me. Other people saw drama everywhere they looked. Wherever I looked, I just saw my Muse for my next drawing or painting. Only now, I had my Muse *and* I saw Sreven.

I went up and surrendered back to my bed, tucked an arm under my head, and stared up at the canopy. I guess I held my breath there a moment until I heard the stairs creak with the weight of his steps as he came up.

I sighed then.

Unexpected— unplanned relief.

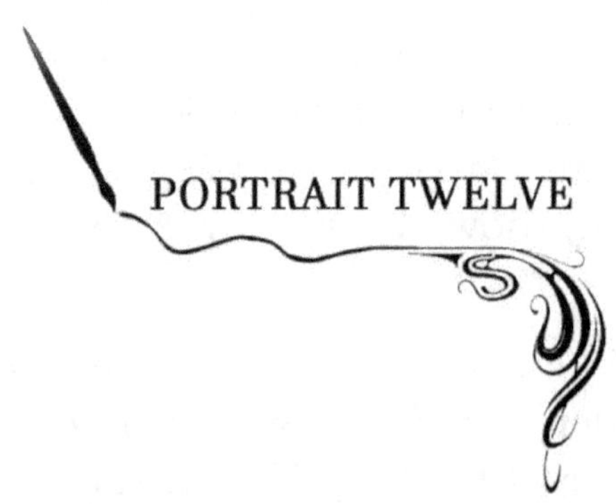

PORTRAIT TWELVE

The guard led us up the stairs, unlocked the door, and then showed us in with a press to his lips that we were to remain quiet. Dimitri and I both nodded complacently.

"You tell Ramone he owes me now," the guard bartered.

"I will and thanks."

"Just don't get caught," he whispered and closed the door behind him.

Turning to look out over the theatre space below, I realized the enclosed balcony we were in wasn't as recessed as I expected it would be. The very exposed feeling had me stepping back further against the wall to keep out of view of those below. Our only benefit was the few lights up here weren't on.

Below, the room was filled with the sections of red theatre seats, touches of gold-umber, and the worst teal-like blue I'd ever seen. Someone should've been shot for the color scheme. Overhead, thick steel beams had been painted to match the same Blood-Orange Red of the seating. The stage was nothing spectacular, just a good broad floor, ideally with plenty of space for a dancer and was presently accommodating a young girl's classical ballet routine to an unfamiliar sonata.

The lighting system was simple with only the basic, black-painted Par-cans and Lekos hanging from black pipes in rows of three, tight up against the rafters, and lit the stage in a wash of frosted white and a watered down blue.

About five rows back from the front, a table riser had been set up over the seats, and the panel of six judges watched with speculative interest.

Dancers were piled in, and some sat or were folded over in the seats, stretching to keep their limbs warmed up. Others lined up along the stage or along the walls, stretching, doing their own version of air guitar dancing while running music in their head, preparing and psyching themselves up for the three minutes they had to show their talents above the others. But no sign of Sreven, and my stomach churned that he may not have come.

"I don't see him," Dimitri panic whispered.

"Shhh."

"He didn't wash out, did he?"

"Shhh."

"But it's killing me."

"Alan Wales!" The name for the next dancer was called out. The name Sreven was borrowing for today. And after far too many heart pounding seconds, he finally stepped out from backstage, looking only a slightly lighter shade of green than I felt.

One of the judges leaned forward in his seat, to peer across the stage at the man who'd just stepped out at the call of another man's name. "You're not Alan." It was, after all, hard to miss, given Alan was African American while Sreven was without a doubt an American shade of the European Caucasian variety.

"I am today." He grinned at them. Another of the panelists nodded and the questioning judge in turn nodded to Sreven.

"Proceed."

Sreven took a few steps back, and the music was cued from someone backstage. Three notes into the melody and I recognized the tune, and I knew I was glad I wasn't going to miss this. Sreven had never told me which song he was going to use, only that he had asked to borrow some. I'd given him a flash drive, with about twenty songs to pick from, based on the ones he'd liked listening and dancing to at my place. I suspected he didn't know which song he was going to settle on either. But playing now was the top pick of them all. *World Without End by Brand X Music.*

Damn, I was fucking glad I was here.

There was a short slow tempo intro, far shorter than the original, but it worked, as it was a very low beat and too much of it would have been demeaning for the importance of today.

A few flowing moves with arms rising up and back over his shoulders. Never rushing and certainly keeping everyone wondering what his performance was truly going to deliver, and then the music kicked in to a dramatic mélange of orchestra and rock music that spoke both of adventure, battles, and lamenting expressions. It was brilliant, but then so was how Sreven's body put the music into motion using his physique.

Sreven launched out toward the downstage edge in an aerial split then landed, only briefly, before he dropped down in a reverse push up— a solid plank of body muscle thrown down to the floor— then sprang back up and launched off the floor and away from the audience in a double axel.

Time froze as I witnessed each movement as an individual spectacle, and how each dance step somehow merged into the next voltaic and liquid. An epic saga of war and journeys all summed up in a 5-turn backspin then a back-launching kick that was the opening into a twist that launched into an aerial pinwheel kick.

The strum of music intensified, bringing with it moods of peril.

Sreven dropped to his knees and went into several Russian leg crawls, crisscrossing to the left, then the right, then a spin on his knees, then up to his feet. His arms swept around, arcing up over his head, like thunder rolling over mountains bringing with it wrath.

Muscles and veins popped in his shoulders, arms, and neck with intense expressions. Legs stretched out and reached, stepped and then launched off the floor again. Suddenly, the battle of music came to a crescendo and paused for a singular heart beating moment.

Sreven's movements slowed to match the sound, his arms drifting towards the floor. He stepped and his back foot rose up slowly, like the second hand to a clock, until his balance tipped him over, placing one hand on the floor as his feet came up overhead in a handstand. His left arm tucked neatly up his side. Then he began to shift his weight. Legs pivoted to one side while his free arm moved in the opposite direction to counter balance. The beat kicked back up, Sreven's legs dropped in a full out split, then his waist twisted and his legs locked in a V, spiraled around, and dropped him into a back walk.

Every movement was as powerful as the tempo of the orchestral rock music, accentuated in a spectacularly unruly balance of style. A cup of contemporary ballet, a heaping tablespoon of Parkour acrobatics, a smidgen of street dancing, spiced up with a dash of stripper for good measure.

The music built up for a climactic finish and Sreven became the slave tossed about the stage in a storm of emotions that lifted and tossed him until finally dropping him towards the downstage edge in a crouched position before a captivated audience. There was a flirting beat, like the tick— tick— tick— of a suspenseful cliffhanger.

But then the music shot into an explosive release, from a ball of mass energy, Sreven launched off the floor in an impossible lift— one foot completely tucked underneath him as his right leg unfolded and catapulted his body up and back off the top of his foot. The music ended— up there in the air with him. Arms raised up in a bitter pose and that one foot pointed right at his judges.

When he came down, there was no thrown head, no power point of toes or frozen arm positions— just the man landing on one foot, the other sliding around to relax behind him— and Sreven looked straight at the judges, for his finale had been the aerial feat and he made no further movements to erase that.

"Damn," the word sputtered out like a gasp breaking loose of my lungs.

"What?" Dimitri whispered from somewhere behind me.

"I think I just came."

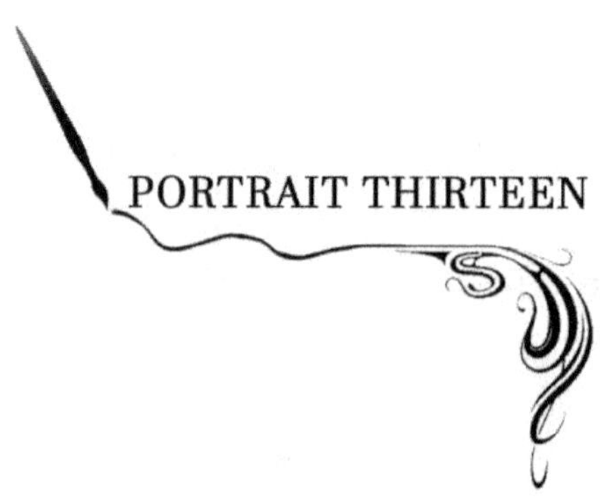

PORTRAIT THIRTEEN

It took some motivation, mostly in the form of money, to get my taxi to put a rush on our errand, but I managed to get what I needed, and returned before the hopeful dancers were released from the tryouts. Namely, my Sreven.

"What are you doing here?" Sreven asked, looking none the victorious as I felt he should.

I stepped up with a bright smile on my face and flowers in my hand. "I bet you were magnificent."

He wasn't so easily convinced, "You can't possibly say that, you weren't there."

Well— I smirked, "I bet you were magnificent," I repeated myself with the same amount of captivation I felt the first time I said it and I pushed the flowers into his hand.

He surrendered to a smile and my open arms. "I doubt the judges think that, but thank you. I needed to hear that."

I received a pretty damn good kiss for it as well.

"Don't you have work?"

"Yes, but I thought you could walk me to work, and perhaps somewhere along the way you could wine and dine me."

"How so?" He looked about as puzzled then as he did our first night together, and I turned and pointed to the picnic basket waiting on the stone wall next to us.

"Jeez, you're an enigma," Sreven practically exacerbated the issue as we walked hand in hand down the block and vanished into Central Park in search of a good picnic spot.

We did, of course, find one under a shady tree along the bank of Turtle Pond. The Weeping Willow was nice, the ducks not so much. But the small grassy knoll was partially closed in with a line of large live oaks, which gave some semblance of privacy. Nevertheless, one can only expect so much living in New York, but it also allowed me to reenact a more homoerotic version of one of master painter, Mark Arian's, romantic realist paintings. *Without* my companion getting all grabby hands with me, *which* he was apt to do given the opportunity, so half my fun was keeping him frustratingly at arm's length. He was super cute when he didn't get what he wanted. It was even more exciting when I dropped the pole leash, letting him move in for the attack. Feel free to insert a *rawr* here if you like. I usually do.

Oh yes, yes, quite right, the picnic— of course, I hadn't the faintest idea what foods, beyond wine and cheese, were considered sexy or romantic. So, two philly cheese steak sandwiches it was, hold the onion and green peppers. Extra cheese.

Not a great match for the red wine either. But Sreven didn't seem to mind my failure to get either right.

After eating the dreadful basket of food, Sreven sat back against the tree and I laid back, taking up Sreven's lap as my pillow.

"So, tell me about your job at the museum."

"I'm one of two exhibit designers."

"What does that mean?" His fingers started lazily comb through my hair as we talked. *Highly recommended here, very relaxing.*

"I'm in charge of overseeing guest exhibits. How they get arranged, color schemes, if and who they might share space with. And I am hands on with the hanging or placement, which can sometimes seem like a game of Tetris."

"And your friend, Dimitri?"

I grinned, "Dimitri is the first preparator that wasn't driven insane by me. That makes him a fantastic assistant and employee. As well as a job savior for me."

Sreven grinned, "How so?"

"I'd gone through— hmmm, six, by the time Dimitri was promoted up. He's been with me ever since, and I haven't been written up as seemingly unruly, overbearing, or for being an impossible-to-work-with monster since then either."

"Maybe you've changed for the better?"

"No. I am still impossible to work with. It's because Dimitri has a *swishi-ness* to him. My peremptory anal retentiveness beads up and rolls right off him like raindrops off a raincoat."

"You spend a lot of time trying to convince me you're an ass, but I don't see it."

I grew serious a moment. Not because I wanted to scare Sreven off, but because I didn't want him to be disillusioned by me either, "Get in the way of me and my work and you'll find a side you've never seen before."

His hand in my hair paused and he looked nearly stunned, more than I had aimed for, "I'm not sure how to take that."

"Imagine how you would feel if someone were to come to the Pumping Station and just got up on the stage and started changing things, or just interfered while you were up there performing."

"I'd get pretty pissed."

"Precisely, so when I have someone who is supposed to assist me instead starts taking apart displays, I have already arranged, or argues with me on my decisions or ignores my designs, I can get right ugly about it. It's not a democracy."

Sreven relaxed then, finding whatever understanding he gained in that last relevance, and his fingers went back to playing in my hair.

"I'm also overbearingly OCD."

"That I had discovered," Sreven laughed and just then his phone rang. He quickly pulled it out then stalled.

"It's them."

"Then answer it."

"But what if—"

"Answer it!" I pushed up feeling some anxiety-*slash*-excitement with him.

He huffed at me but did so, "Hello?" He paused, "Yes, this is he."

And then the *llloonnng* pause—

Are you on the edge of your seat? Good. I just wanted to make sure you suffered that moment as I had. As it was excruciatingly painful not to just blurt out a disruptive '*Well?*' at him while he was still on the phone, getting whatever details of adoration or *we liked you but—*

There's always the *but* in the letdown. The passive aggressive rejection. Why can't they just come out and say you sucked and we decided to go with the one who sucked less, or you both sucked but the other one is cuter. Of course, in Sreven's case, he didn't suck and he was also the cuter one. Yes, yes, just throw it in my face that I am far from being biased, or that good looks is a speculative admiration. However, I also knew a good thing when I saw—

"I made the first cut."

"As if there was ever any doubt." I shared a beaming grin with him.

If Sreven had intended to get a new dose of nervous wreckage at that moment, I had successfully deflated it, at least for the moment, because I saw it go with a quick exhale and a refreshed smile, and he quickly leaned in for a kiss, "You're too good for my ego. Do you know that?"

I wasn't given the chance for an answer as the intruding kiss-stealer closed in. Quickly followed up with grabby-hands being added in on the embrace. I can only say this— thank goodness there aren't any utility closets in Central Park or I might not have ever made it into work on time that day.

It was definitely a good day. Fresh air, the sun shining down on my skin— *the parts that weren't being petted*. A fed belly. A beautiful man, who was both boyishly innocent in face and nefariously hedonistic body, pressed against me. And all that combined from this one afternoon, gifted me enough fuel to feed my Muse that would unfailingly keep me going for a couple of weeks.

Not to forget, the kiss that was trying terribly so to not get too rambunctious would have me on the edge for sexual need for just as long. *Grrrrrrrr*— and that's what I have to say about that.

"What's next now?" I forced the kiss to break between us. I needed air and my cock needed to come down off cloud nine.

"Now we work as a troupe with various choreographers. I come in every day for the next nine days or until I get cut."

I ran my fingers down the side of his face, looking up at him, but my eyes were already seeing him tomorrow and the next day, watching him step, turn, and lock.

"What?" his face crimped, perplexing my far away amusements.

"Nothing. I need to get to work. So, when does this troupe stuff start?" I couldn't wipe the smile from my lips. That is, until Sreven had the nerve to suggest he wasn't going.

"Doesn't matter. I'm not going."

I couldn't believe I was hearing this yet again. "You're going. It doesn't matter if you make all nine days or just one, what matters is that you show up as instructed."

Sreven sat back, looking far more frustrated than I might have expected him to look. He sucked in a deep breath, his eyes glancing away, and he leaned back against the tree as before and shook his head some more. "I mean, I can't."

"Why can't you?" I pushed up on my hands to sit up to look at him.

"I lost a lot of money just taking time off work so I could prepare. But my rent is coming due. I can't afford to take another nine days off or even half that."

It was risky, but I'd seen him at his best now and decided it was worth it, "Why don't you let me help you with your rent, then."

"I don't want this to be about needing a hand-out."

"Oh, cut me some slack here. I'm proficient in ass-ism, remember? I'll just make you put out extra in exchange," I laughed, but the ploy didn't work. He was clearly on the downward slump. "How much is it anyways?"

"Fifteen hundred." He winced.

I'm not sure how long I must have sat there like a lump on a log. A grand and a half in New York was nothing. In fact, you can't even rent a dumpster for that much. "Whose two hundred year-old grandpappy did you knock off to get that kind of rent?"

Sreven finally laughed, "Not me. I have two roommates. Shelly got the place from her ex-boyfriend when he moved to Europe or something. She pays the larger portion, and Trevor and I each pay fifteen each."

"Ah, okay, now it all makes since. So, good. I can handle fifteen."

"How the hell do you have that kind of spare cash lying around?"

"I sold several paintings back at the museum's fundraiser gala, remember? It's funny how I get to keep some of that."

"Hey, speaking of that night. You ever gonna tell me what the deal was about the couple you were talking to when we came out of the closet?"

The chuckle got away from me— out of the closet indeed. "That stupefied couple had been none other than my mother and father."

"Your parents?" His expression blanched, "Why didn't you—" he fell silent a moment, his eyes the windows of his memory replaying that night, "I'm confused."

"I hadn't seen them in over ten years."

"That sucks."

"Not at all. It was by my choice."

"Any brothers or sisters?"

"Brothers. Six actually."

"Do you ever see them?"

"No, they are the effigies of our father. It was only I who failed in that regress."

"It must feel lonely being rejected by your entire family, though."

"I was lonelier when I was growing up inside it. My parents weren't the affectionate type. If you did something good, our father would give us a glance of pride and say, *'Excellent'*, before walking off. I think one of my brothers claimed to have gotten a pat on the shoulder once. None of us believed him."

"You never thought it was weird?"

"My parents never touched. They even slept in separate rooms. We didn't see anything to know it was missing. There was this one box, I found." The thought brought a curl to my lips. "However—" I'd grown tiresome of memory lane and changed the subject back to that of rent and victory, "running into them that night was rather victorious for me. So, to celebrate, let me cover your rent so that your event can be victorious too."

A soft smile fought its way onto his lips in small micro twitches until finally it was visible. The shadows of doubt evaporated in the summer warmth as the sun started to make its way down the western sky, "Okay, but you have to let me work it off somehow. Let me pay you back for some of it, at least."

"Don't worry, I will make a list. Starting payment, I need a chaperone to see me safely to the Metro and then a kiss good night would be most *auspendious*."

"Auspeh- what? Is that even a word?"

I grinned. "It is now."

Sreven's brows furrowed, his eyes narrowing suspiciously. "I don't get it."

I pushed up and casually began to pack up our picnic affairs. "Ever find it funny how a dancer, such as yourself, can invent or combine movements to create new dance steps, and a painter, as I am amply inclined to call myself, can mix up new colors with paint, yet an author is ridiculed if they make up words to fit an act or emotion when they are unable to find a genuine word to properly describe it?" I shrugged then stood with the basket on one arm and pulled Sreven up to join me. "It hardly makes any sense, especially when no one puts up a fuss about the slang each new generation creates in their youth. I'd preferably hand the task over to the wiser penmanship of the wordy artists. Language all together, I think, would evolve far better with the novelists and poets. I mean, seriously, how have words such as yolo, twerk, or swerve elevated our culture?"

"Oh, come on now, you chirping on twerking?"

My head snapped around to eye him, and he had that look of purposeful trouble-making written all over his face. So defined, his eyes flared with naughtiness. I met them with a broody scowl, "Mark my words, the demise of society is being fast forwarded because the two words you just used will reach the dictionary before mine will."

PORTRAIT FOURTEEN

On the fourth day at the try out, Sreven got cut. And he was a little happier for it as he called to talk about how Alan and I had been right and he'd been approached from a few talent scouts. The highlight of his call was to let me know he was coming over to warm my sheets up for me.

The night following, Sreven returned to his familiar world of pole dancing at the Pumping Station and I got back to my paintings.

In the weeks that followed, give or take a few days, we'd only spoken a few times on the phone. Sreven was working every night, making up for lost time and income. He had some crazy notion that he was going to try to pay off some of the cash I had given him. Such nonsense. But it did me some good. I had four empty slots in my collection since the gala. And painting while wearing a Sreven horny skin suit was not co-productive in the way of producing paintings. Well— except for that once, and I still had that one.

I'd just finished one of the paintings I had planned last night and was browsing through the forest of canvases, letting them talk to me and letting me know which one I would be starting on next, when I got a call.

"Hello?"

"Uh, yeah, is Xherdan Chantal in?"

"You got 'im."

"Oh, awesome. Hey, this is Giannis Papas. We met a few months ago when you wanted me to come by for a modeling session."

"Give me an image please." Names meant nothing to me— it was all about what I saw.

"I'm part Greek, muscular build with heavy guns. We met at a concert where I was working as the bodyguard for a singer—"

"Yes, now I remember you. Long, wavy black hair and a trimmed beard around your chin. You had a nice neck if I remember right." My Muse perked up at the thought of a pose with neck veins popping with head and shoulders tossed back in anguish, hidden in a brooding storm of dark colors. A nice change of pace from the athlete piques of interest I'd been indulging in lately. "But you were on tour and couldn't do it then."

"That's me. Say, I know this is kind of sudden and last minute, but any chance you're available tonight? I got a couple weeks break right now, but I'd told my girl about it, and she's rather turned on by it. Absence doesn't always make the heart grow fonder. You know what I mean?"

No. I hadn't a clue about such things. Nor did I care. Not about hearts or fondness. But having a shot to feed the man on the other side of the phone to my Muse was a definite yes. "As a matter of fact, I am open this evening. Want to make it around seven?"

"Yes, and it's okay Helena comes with me, right?"

"To watch? Sure. Might even ask her to join you if the chemistry is right."

"Don't say that where she can hear you. Or you'll never have the chance to take it back," the man on the other end of the line laughed, *"What's the address?"*

"129 Chrystie Street. You'll see a loading dock, then a small roll up door to the right. Next to it is a set of steps with a grey door. It looks like it's part of the grey apartments, but it's not. Just ring and I'll let you in."

Modeling isn't the glamorous thing most people think it is. Someone stands on the set. I take pictures. Sometimes when they pose, their bodies look awkward or stiff. Sometimes I can get them to relax. Music often helps, but then it has to be my kind of music not theirs, so that has the possibility of backfiring at times. This night was one of them and we went without music all together. Modern pop music was only tolerable on a dance floor for equal grounds of groping.

Giannis worked his clothes off little by little as we went. He had a tendency to move his hands to play wherever they landed. Clearly this man had a different agenda with the modeling. Using it as some form of eye candy foreplay for his woman. Which brought my shot more on the erotic side. *Fine by me. My Muse had need for both: with and without. So did my audience.* And Giannis had a body to satisfy a manly type need for most. The chemistry between him and his woman could have given Mount Vesuvius a run for its money, and I was soon asking her to join Giannis in the poses.

"Are you comfortable so far?" I asked Helena, just to be sure the session wasn't crossing a line with her. I rarely worked with women and that was cause for an underlining fear that all this could be misconstrued and received as pornography could ruin the vibes my Muse pulled from, especially if it came to surface for my modeling subjects. But she gave me a most deviously wicked grin and nodded her compliance.

It seemed I was the only one on the nervous side. "Good. I'd like to get a few more shots of the two of you together, then just a few more of just him before we're finished here, if you don't mind."

"Not at all. Where do you want me?" Helena asked with a charming relaxed air that was refreshing.

"Giannis, if you'd stand up facing the backdrop. Helena, you come around behind him and face his back. Then I want you both to raise your arms up in a Y—" I waited until they were both in position. Helena's shorter height put her head almost perfectly at the center of his back. An alignment easily fixed by having her stand on a photo album. "Okay. Helena, bend your arms inward so they come under his, then rest your hands on the back of his head. Giannis, bring your hands in and rest them so they almost overlap hers." I reached in and micro-managed the placement just so. I turned Helena's head to place her cheek to his spine, then stepped back and snapped off a few shots.

"Helena, drop your left arm down and place your hand on his thigh. Giannis, drop your left arm down by your side, then reach back and place your palm to the curve of Helena's hip. Then turn your face to look straight off your left shoulder." I snapped a few more, "One more pose together and then you can get dressed, Helena. Giannis, I want you to turn around then step into Helena so your bodies are seamless, but then lean back and drop your head. Helena, lean into him with your ear to his sternum and left hand to his bicep. Giannis, your right hand under her arm and on her shoulder blade." I waited until they were in position. Now tense your muscles." The moment they did, I had the image I had been searching for all night. *It was perfect.*

"Yessss, thank you." I reached for the terry robe draped over the stool and handed it to Helena, "Thank you, again."

She merely gave me another one of those wicked grins and the glimmer in her eye said all that I had just captured in the last pose.

"Just a few more of you, Giannis." I snapped a few more while Helena disappeared into the bathroom to get dressed.

Giannis looked down at his body and his thickening cock, then gave me a sheepish grin, "Even with this?"

"Precisely with that." I hid my grin behind the viewfinder of my camera and focused in, "Drop down to both knees and sit back on your heels." I snapped as he moved, "That's it. Now, spread your knees a little wider. Then sit back on your heels with your right hand on the floor behind you." I watched him get in position, "Up on your fingertips, please. Perfect. Now drop your head back." I stepped in to adjust the thick mop of black hair, making sure at least one of Giannis's ringlets was clearly made out on his shoulder, then stepped back and clicked off a few shots. It was a perfect ending to the session. So, when I heard the door down below open, I tossed Giannis a towel, "We're all done. Thank you very much."

I turned away, turning the view screen to the camera on to browse through my productive night as I blindly walked towards the sliding door to greet my surprise visitor.

"Sreven." I let my surprise show when the door rolled to the side and my beautiful hedonist stepped in. Hmmm, maybe the paintings could wait a bit. I welcomed him with a peck then turned, heading back to the studio, still browsing the collection of images on the camera.

"What's going on?"

I shot a glance over my shoulder at Sreven and smiled, "Giannis was in town, so I had him come over for a photo shoot." I stopped at my desk and dropped down on the edge, letting one leg dangle while still flipping through the screen and trashing a few bad shots.

"Did you now?" Sreven stepped up beside me, and I grinned as I watched him watch the enticing Greek male get dressed. It was precisely the reason I had sought a shoot with the man. Giannis just had a solid allure to him that both men and women were drawn to. I wondered how long it would take from the moment my Muse's subjects left until Sreven would be pouncing on me with demands to take him down to the floor. Yeah, I sighed, the painting would definitely have to wait.

A moment later, stepping out from the third bedroom was Helena. She prowled up to Giannis with a sultry step and rolled up on her toes to plant a kiss to his cheek, showing the foreplay had worked its magic on her. "I may have to beg Xherdan to use you more often. That was sexy as hell." She winked at me.

Which planted a smile on my face. But I got what I needed. And it was rare for me to call the same model back. But I soon lost my smile when I felt the back of Sreven's hand smack me against the arm. I twisted, shooting him a *what the fuck* glare, only to be met with a scowl of his own.

I did my best to show some form of silent warning glance, but it was doubtful Sreven was registering it. His brows near stitched together at the center, his jaw biting down. He was ready to fight over something. *Guess I was back to painting tonight.*

I glanced at the last photo, now displayed on the camera's view screen, showing Giannis sitting back on his heels, his cock jutting out from his body, and his head thrown back, letting his black waves fall down over his shoulder and back. The images even more vivid in my mind, still burning in my head like succulent pastries just waiting to be sampled, and I really wanted to get started on my painting.

Giannis was finally dressed and walked up, "Thanks again for the experience." He reached out and we shook hands. I handed over an envelope of cash for his time, which he waved playfully, "I'm treating her with this." He wiggled his eyebrows, then wrapped one of those luxuriously muscled arms around her frame and escorted her out.

No sooner had the door slid closed when Sreven came around for a face off and the rage was nothing short of hell burning away in his eyes.

"What the fuck was all that?!"

"A modeling shoot. What did you think it was?" I wasn't matching might for might.

"Naked?"

I must admit the accusation was a straight pitch at me; after all, nearly all the physiques I drew or painted were *yes— naked*. This point of contention had me more than flummoxed. I just couldn't understand it. I didn't even bother to answer, it was so ridiculous.

"So, that's how this is going to go?"

"How is what going? Try calming down a moment and think about what you're saying because I'm not sure myself."

"I come over and find you up here with another man."

"Again, he was modeling for me."

"And you didn't think to bring it up to me beforehand?"

"There was no *beforehand*. He called earlier to see if I had time and I said yes." I shrugged my shoulders, seeing no relevance for this to be made an issue.

"And that's all that happened?"

I handed the camera over, so he could see for himself, "Hit the arrow button to scroll through."

Sreven wrenched his shoulder, taking the camera with him, but where I thought my work should have dispelled whatever was burning in his mind clearly was detonating his anger further instead. I watched as Sreven's body grew tauter. His shoulders and back heaved with deep seething breaths, and the next thing I saw— was my camera going flying across the studio.

"WHAT THE FUCK?!?!" I jumped to my feet, reaching out to catch Sreven and spin him about. Again, he jerked away, avoiding contact.

"I can't fucking believe you brought someone else to your place." Sreven leered at me.

I was clearly at a disadvantage here. And I headed across the floor in search of my camera. I wasn't used to arguments. I had no experience in them. Or in seeing anything I had done would warrant one, "What the fuck, Sreven? I'm a painter, this is what I do." I waved my hands up to accentuate the warehouse space, "And this is where I work. This isn't a fucking hobby. Having models come here to pose is no different than you dancing for your audience."

Sreven was hot on my heels with his comeback, "My audience doesn't come to my home."

"Mine do." I bent over, glanced under one of the tables, then moved on to the next.

"Why must they?!"

"Because this is where my studio is?"

"But I would have thought since we were dating, you wouldn't be bringing anyone else around to snap off shots and fuck."

I stopped at the next table and spun around to look at Sreven, "Fuck? Where did fucking come into this?"

"IF NOT TO FUCK, THEN WHY WAS HE HERE!?!" Sreven bellowed, tossing his arms out wide.

"TO MUSE ME ONLY!" I roared back.

Fuck, I hated fighting. What a waste of energy, but this was about to go a distance that would alter our course and there would be no coming back from it once it crossed that line. Perhaps some of his fire was squelched, but none of mine. If he said it again, there would be only one response left from me. And sadly, Sreven went there.

"Don't give me that muse bullshit. If I hadn't shown up? Then what? You would have fucked your muse like you fucked me?"

"Get out!" I pitched. The air between us fused cold as ice in a snap. Not even the raging anger Sreven had been slinging at me could melt the chill I now felt. For the moment he vocalized his jealousy of my Muse, it eroded away everything between us.

"What?" Clearly, he hadn't calculated his jealous raging would reach such an effect of severity.

"You heard me—" I stopped thinking. There was only frigid resentment in me now. He'd accused me of such things without any grounds. More so, the animosity stemmed from him to dare step between me and my artwork. I shoved forward, keeping him in my grip. "Get out— Get Out— GET OUT!" I pushed him for the door.

"No wait." He was suddenly resisting the direction I had him going in.

I released part of my hold on his shirt so I could grab the sliding panel, jerked it open, and then hustled Sreven out by the scruff of his jacket, then closed the freight door back into its place.

Sreven was instantly pounding from the other side, but I would have none of him coming back in to carry on further, so I kicked the drop pin into its hole to lock him out.

I turned my back to the pounding and just stood there, feeling the cold sweats break out across my back and shoulders. I listened to his boots go down the stairs, the front door swinging open, only to slam shut and followed with an anguished, "*FUCK!*" called out from the sidewalks below.

It ripped me in half and tore my breath from my lungs.

Paint. Just go fucking paint and forget the rest. I stormed past the tempera table, grabbed up several cups, and mixed out a few paint colors like a wild man. After I snatched up a handful of brushes, I climbed up on the scaffolding to the first blank canvas. I loaded the camel hairs of a brush with a poorly mixed Bronze Blue then froze. I just stood there and boiled. I should have been able to burn holes into the canvas the way I felt, but what I wasn't seeing was the man I had intended to paint.

All that energy and vibe from the photo shoot was gone.

I let out a heavy disgruntled sigh and dropped the brush to my feet, then the cup, not caring where it splattered.

And then the surge boiled over and ran its course, "GOD DAMMIT! WHY?!?!" My outburst echoed off the brick mortar of the walls and died away. I glanced around and spotted my camera lying in the aisle between the canvas stations, so I climbed down to go after it. Maybe I could salvage some of tonight.

The body casing was split on one side and its lens hung at a broken angle from the locking ring. It was definitely a goner, but as long as the chip inside was good— I turned it over, finding the view screen shattered, and after several attempts to get the camera to pull up the display, all that came up on the screen were ribbons of spattered pixelated data. It was ruined and everything from the shoot was lost.

I felt a fresh surge of anger and spun, sending the camera flying across the studio like a cannonball, and then I heard the pop and rip. I snapped around and was met with horror.

My masterpiece sitting at the far end now bore the injury of a hole right in its center.

In the following couple of seconds, as I stared at the destruction, everything left me, even my soul fled me, for I was unworthy of keeping it. I crumpled, then fell to my knees and folded over to surrender my head to my hands on the floor. My Muse gone and now my one true masterpiece— destroyed.

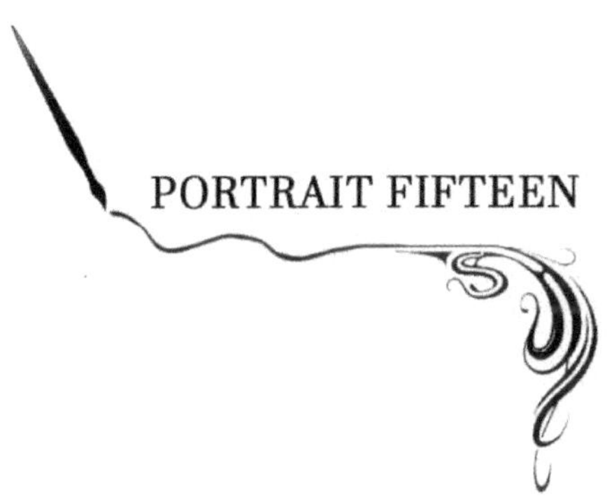

PORTRAIT FIFTEEN

"Crates are in place and waiting for you." Tom poked his head in my office where Dimitri and I sat while I glanced over the evening itinerary sheet.

I nodded at Tom. "Thanks." Then waved to my padawan to indicate it was time to go.

"Is there something wrong?" Dimitri asked as we headed out. He'd asked the very same question every night this week. And so far, my answer had remained no.

"What makes you ask?" I tried a new tactic to divert the question away.

"You seem different."

"No, I don't.

"Yeah— you do."

"No— I don't." I started for the stairs.

Dimitri stopped, reluctant to follow. "Can we please do the European arrivals last?" He gave me a nervous look.

I stopped at the ballast, one foot already on the first step, and turned to glance at him. "And risk my mood worsening in the night?"

"See? I told you something was wrong." He let out a heavy surrendering sigh. We headed upstairs toward the paintings where eleven new arrivals awaited to be hung in place. And if Dimitri was lucky, both laser levels would have been brought out and awaiting us to ease the pain.

The new paintings, unlike our usual touring arrivals, were waiting in a slotted rack, tagged from the catalog department, for these were coming to join the permanent collection of the Metropolitan.

The first two were going up in the Renaissance Gallery. I climbed up the ladder at our first opening and made a few faint chalk marks on the wall, measured down from the ceiling, then took measurements of the height of the frame from the first painting. The rest was rudimentary and boring. It was simply mechanical involvements to get the painting to stick to the wall. What came next was, according to Dimitri's definition, an evil plot to drive him crazy as I stepped away and we began the anal retentive, obsessive compulsive disorder battle that the finite difference was all due to one's personal imbalance of testicle position while looking that could have taken the tyrannical reigns from the likes of Napoleon all in the name of ensuring the painting was perfectly and unequivocally to the lesser degree of a nano hair cell— level.

"Do you want to talk about it?" Dimitri asked from atop the ladder as he tapped the right side of the painting for the twentieth time or so per my instructions.

The very question broke me from my seething focus on the painting, which may have inevitably saved the artifact from utter ruin as I was staring more at the painted brush strokes of a body draped over a sofa within the paintings rather than at the actual alignment of the frame itself on the wall. My thoughts heedingly dark and brooding, trying to burn a hole in what I saw. *Because what I saw was a painting that was crooked within the frame!*

"About?" I forced my attention back to the task at hand and motioned him to tweak the frame to the left some more.

"About what's bothering you."

I knelt down to change my viewing perspective on the frame. "What makes you think something is bothering me?" I motioned him to tap it to the right.

"Because you've been walking around here like some brooding thunder clap with a broken heart for the last four days."

"That is the most ridiculous thing I've heard, Dimitri. You, of all people, know one must be in love to experience a broken heart."

"Yes, and—"

"And nothing." I took a step back, still not satisfied. "The frame must be crooked. It will be impossible to get this level."

I don't know what Dimitri was thinking he was going to prove when he pointedly, applying emphasis on his finger and the evil he was about to commit, landed the assaulting finger on the frame and, just began to push it off its tilt.

I just stood there and deliberated some more, waiting for him to finish with his little game. "I can do this all night," I warned.

He rolled his eyes, but stopped, knowing full well I could. Chances were good we would be anyways and I pointed him to tap it back to the right— times a dozen more taps.

Finally, only a second shy of an hour later, I declared myself satisfied with the first hang of the night, and we moved on to the next painting needing to go up. Same thing, just a few spots further down the hall.

"Do you want to know what I think?" my Padawan made the adjustment to the painting then to his queer man-package.

I ignored the question along with his flippant suggestive motioning, and pointed him to move the frame.

"I think you and Sreven have broken up for some reason and you're hurting from it."

Again, I said nothing and pointed him to move the painting until satisfied, then we moved on to the next. This time adding a seventieth century Dutch portrait to the Robert Lehman sitting room Gallery.

"I take it you've been listening to people who have no business gossiping about me."

"I'm trying to listen to you, but you won't talk to me about it."

I stopped and looked at him because, for the first time, he sounded heartbroken himself.

"Why does it matter? It's over and nothing can be done about it."

"Please don't say that," he nearly sounded like he was begging.

It was touching, but Dimitri had his hopes hung up on the wrong clothesline if I was the hope of romance-kind. I had a lover that felt good. Who seemed to have fit right, no matter what position we took, until he tried to stand between me and my art. The course of retaliation would have been for me to take a chainsaw to all his poles. Which I could never do because I found some catharsis knowing he was inside the Pumping Station, committing spinal suicide on the pole every night. Maybe even doing another one of those jumps. The other reason it never happened was because it just wasn't in me to do the things others did. What justice would I have? It didn't work; at least I found out before I let him move in and sacrificed yet another sofa to a secret pet Cujo-Godzilla.

The last painting to go up threatened to do us both in. A modern abstract of angular shapes also challenged my ability to bite my opinionated lip. I would have preferred Annie the Elephant's work over this. At least with hers, one could treat it like an inkblot card. Illusions that some semblance of shape existed within the painting. In this jumble of splatter paints, one only found a headache that not even the best headache tea could fix. I might have to buy a bottle of Advil for once, when the night was over.

After nearly an hour, with a minor break for Dimitri's sanity, we gave up and when the laser levels said it was level, we walked away. Agreeing that I was barred from the hall from now and until which time a thief came into the night and stole the monstrosity away. Who knows, maybe some Athenian or Aegean hero might need it to battle against Medusa and turn her into stone. The horrid angular claim of modern art might even work too.

We made a round trip to the break room, where we raided Dimitri's lunch box of his grapes and I took a moment to think a little harder on the Advil thing.

"Have you even tried talking to him since?"

"How much of my affair do you actually know, Dimitri?" I meant to glare at him but fell short of the execution. Felt the lack thereof on my face as I looked at him amused by the night-ness of the lavender-fuchsia fusion hair dye, then snatched his grapes away and we headed back out to finish our unpacking.

"Won't you give it another shot?" More pleading.

"Don't suppose you realize it takes two and this scenario is a man short."

"But you could call him or go see him at the club. Something."

"Why?"

"Because you deserve to have someone. Because—
"

"Because what, Dimitri?"

He shrugged and turned away to start opening one of the crates for our next exhibit.

"Dimitri, do not play the *Because* game with me tonight. I haven't the patience for it."

"But you love that game," Dimitri played coy.

I was in no mood for playing, "Don't make me hurt you."

"Because if someone like you can't make a relationship work, what possible chance would I have?"

"What do you mean someone like me? What am I?"

"An artist. A really great artist."

"Being an artist isn't the reason for not getting involved with people."

"Remember what you said about me and Matteo? Now Sreven has done the same thing to you. Got jealous of your muse, I mean."

"It seems I don't need to tell you anything of what happened."

"I think his roommate has been crushing on him for some time; he didn't like Sreven dating you and so I got an earful then. Now he's happy you two broke up. So again—" Dimitri's expression saddened, "I get an earful."

"This roommate? He knows you work with me?"

"And ruin the surprise?"

"And Sreven? Is he happier now?" I regretted asking it the second it came out of my mouth. I didn't need to know if he was miserable. Or capable of moving on without a second thought about me. What I hoped was that he was spinning around his pole or getting calls from dance troupes, or something productive like that. His happiness was not mine to wish harm on.

"I- I don't—"

"Don't answer that." I shook my head and busied myself with the task at hand.

I began pulling the statues out from their packing, bringing them to the center display table for Dimitri to position properly and set their tags in place next to them. "Why do you think I don't get into relationships?" I began, thinking since we'd gone this far, I might as well make the conversation productive and conduct some therapy into the psyche of one Xherdan Chantal and the enigma that I was. *Enigma. Too bad Sreven didn't really believe that,* I sighed.

"Because you're an ass?"

I tried to laugh, but it just wasn't in me. I was an ass, but there was a good reason for it. "Being an ass is just a defense mechanism. A damn good one, too."

"What defenses?" Dimitri was practically up in arms over such claims from me, "You don't ever date anyone or let anyone in."

I shrugged. "Because, when growing up, only to realize the two people in the world who were supposed to love you above all others unconditionally, turned around and burdened you with more conditions and short comings than all the strangers of the world put together. After a revelation like that, you— or well, *I*— felt I didn't want to waste any more parts of my life being tied to more of *that*."

Dimitri didn't know, he knew my parents and I, like many gay men, were not on speaking terms, but it was all he knew. And I could see he felt my pain, it was something we all shared in some form or another, less or more degrees of each, but we all shared in it. "The world is just something I paint. What I don't need is someone judging me for that. Not when they are also lying in my bed or holding my hand."

Dimitri shook his head, taking the next vase from my hands as I passed it over, and I watched as his delicate fingers set it up on its podium. He gave it perhaps a sixteenth of a turn, then glanced at me. The minute shake of my head registered in his actions, as he turned the vase another small degree in the other direction before leaving it be.

"People come together for all kinds of reasons," I started back up while digging out another item from the swamp of shavings inside the crate. "Lust, laughs, crushes, infatuations, curiosity. But never love. Love comes later, and sometimes not at all. And even when it doesn't, some people stay together. They're happy, or are only part happy, or not at all, but they're afraid to be alone or let go. Then someone new comes along, and maybe that new person could have been the right one. The one who you would have discovered love with. Problem is, you don't have space in your life for that new person to enter because you thought it was better to bog yourself down with the one you're still not happy with, all because you were avoiding loneliness."

"Sounds like crap to me."

"Is it?" I stuffed a wad of shavings into Dimitri's hands instead of the next vase.

"What's this?"

"Yesterday's crap." I looked at him flatly, "Now pick up the vase."

Right away, he moved and dropped the shavings. It was as automatic as breathing that I doubt he grasped it, so I made sure he did.

"What did you just do?" I asked, just as he was picking up the seventeenth century cobalt Limoge style vase; its heavily gold gilded features framed a painting of two women in a garden, playing with a couple of cherubs.

"I picked up the vase like you said." He blinked several times, clearly not getting it.

"And what did you do with the stuff that was already in your hands?"

His face wrinkled up and he looked at me like I had truly lost my marbles. To be honest, I may have never had any to start with. Something had to have been out of whack with me in the beginning stages of childhood for me to turn out this way, right? "You dropped them. You have to let go of yesterday's crap. Or, you make room by moving all the shavings to one hand, and hold the vase in the other. But then, you're cheating and it destroys any chance of the new relationship being anything worth keeping. Because, if you cheat on one to be with another, chances are, you'll cheat on them at a time when you start to question or doubt."

"I don't get it."

"Eventually you're going to drop the vase, trying to hold on with just one hand while the other hangs on to the old shavings."

Dimitri suddenly set the vase down and took a step back. *Dropping* was a bad mojo word inside the Metro. I could have talked until I was blue in the face and Dimitri would have never picked the vase up again, so I did. It was my fault, so I took it over to its podium and set it to its new forever home.

"So, you're saying it's better to not date at all?" Dimitri checked the crate, making sure we didn't miss anything, before passing a handful of bolts and wing nut sets to me so I could close the wooden freight box back up.

I slid the lid into place on the crate and dropped the four bolts I had down into the holes, then began spinning the nuts into place as I talked. "How many boyfriends have you had this year?"

Dimitri twisted his mouth while doing the same on his side of the crate with the remaining bolt sets before reluctantly answering, "Eight."

"And of those eight, how many of them did you exchange *I love you's* with?"

Again, his face twitched, growing ever more uncomfortable with his reality, though scrutiny was not the point I was out to make. "Six."

"How many of those were true?"

"What?" Dimitri stammered, and I could see that was something he didn't want to question. Whatever semblance of good he'd gotten or hoped he had was something he didn't want to question and cast doubt on. I decided to spare him.

"My point is people aren't always together for what they think it is or want it to be, they get together to run away from loneliness. But the person they're with is little more than a stranger, yet they don't change it until it becomes a loathsome burden." I shrugged, realizing this was starting to sound too much like a monologue of anti-Romeo Alan Watts gibberish. "I don't eat food I don't like. I don't pretend to be someone or something I'm not. So, why waste time with pretend relationships?"

"And Sreven?"

"I wasn't pretending, I just didn't know what it was, okay?"

"And were you happy with him?"

"I was—" I answered far too quickly but then the inner rage flickered like a new match not willing to be snuffed out just yet. "Up until he picked the wrong fight with me."

Dimitri nodded, and for a moment he looked like he pitied me.

"Come on, we still have the new Pompeii arrivals to set up downstairs."

We returned all the packing material back to the other two crates we had emptied and closed them up. Dimitri pulled out a roll of large red stickers and slapped one to each of the crates to let maintenance know they were ready to go back to holding until it was time for another piece of artwork to bid farewell and adieu and shipped off for a new city and a new audience of onlookers.

"By the way, I have a whole new shipment of tempera coming in a few days, why don't you come over and help me make the mixes. I'll let you make up a few batches to take home for yourself, if you like."

"Really?"

"Really, really."

"You miss him, don't you?"

"Why do you say that?"

"Because, you never invite company over except to muse you for your work."

It was my turn to twitch, and I didn't bother to either confess or deny it.

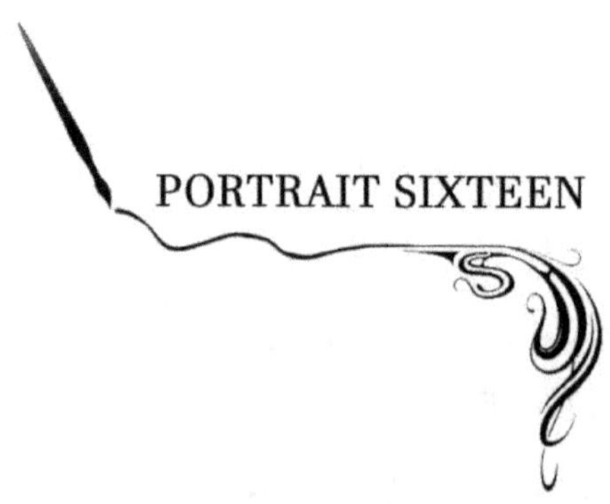

PORTRAIT SIXTEEN

"Why is your sofa on the sidewalk with serial killer Louis Fitonnio sitting on it?" my arrival asked as he let himself in.

I didn't even get the chance to explain when the high-pitched squeal was broadcasted from Dimitri's lips to my walls as he raced over to the new sofa and pounced on it. "I can't believe you finally broke down and got a new sofa." He ran his fingers over the brocade upholstery like it was fur, "Red. I love red. You bought a red sofa." His eyes stopped on something, then he pointed to the remnants of a stain and gaped up at me, "Is that what I think it is?"

I only shook my head and laughed at him, "It's just a sofa, now take off your shoes and come help me."

"Take off— have you gone mental or something?"

"No, and it's bad luck to prep paints with shoes on. Take them off."

"Since when? I didn't take off my shoes last time."

"Yeah, and look where it landed me."

"Dimitri Charming is not going to walk barefooted on your nasty warehouse floors."

"Take them off or go back home." I turned my back to him to end the disagreement. I could feel the scowl on the back on my head, but I soon heard the clunk of two shoes hit the floor and not a sound as he made his way over to join me at the tempera table. On the floor were several stacked boxes, and we cut into them and began the task of putting the fresh tinted powders into their assigned wooden troughs.

"Save a couple of those boxes for you to take some paints home."

"I don't need any, but thanks."

I stopped in mid scoop and glanced at him, noting the sullen features of my padawan. "What's the matter?"

He shrugged.

"You know, your muse is more likely to pick up if it has media supplies to work with."

Another shrug from his bony, slender shoulders.

I handed over several 3x5 cards. Each painted over on one side with a color shade and on the backside the recipe for the color. "Take those and start mixing the dried ingredients I need for each."

He nodded compliance.

"When was the last time you painted something?"

Another shrug.

"Dimitri."

"I just don't think painting is the right medium for me now."

"You're just saying that to excuse the rut."

"No. I just—" he trailed off. Something was bothering him, and like most times, it was hard to get it out of him. I know what you're thinking. You're thinking I shouldn't expect anything less, given me as his role model? My response is— I didn't teach him this rotten pet trick.

"Just what? Want a head of cabbage for dinner? Sorry, all out. I do, however, have several canvasses that don't like talking to me right now, so if you want so lay claim to one, just speak up. You just can't have that one."

Dimitri's face snapped up and looked at me, though I was busy mixing tinctures, "What one?"

I glanced up, keeping my face as flat lined as I could. "That one."

His eyes darted to the forest, then back. "Which one?"

"Yes."

He scowled. I laughed. He pouted. But that's when he started talking while his long fingers scooped out some of the Egyptian umber and dropped it into a cup. "I really want to just focus on drawing and sketching instead."

"Really? So why don't you?"

"Because the pencils cost more than the paints do."

"Which pencils?"

"Pastels."

"Why did I not see this coming? Watercolor pastels by chance?"

"Oh, yes, those too." His face brightened. "I love drawing something out, then splattering it with water, but I can't afford them." He screwed up his lips. He pressed a lid down on the cup he'd just finished mixing, marked it, then set it aside.

Later with the boxes emptied, the color cards mixed and set aside, Dimitri wandered off from the table, returned to the sofa, and dropped down on it.

"Dating anyone new?" I asked across the room. Not because Dimitri's present love life interested me, but because I saw his attention going to an object under the sofa. I would have rather he didn't get curious, but my inquiry did little to jump his track, and I soon saw my hideaway sketch pad being pulled out from under the sofa and into Dimitri's lap.

I felt a small pang of regret because I knew what the tablet contained. More than two dozen various charcoal sketches— every one of them of the same physique. Never before had I dedicated an entire pad of paper to one person. Never had one person taken up my thoughts as he had.

I dismissed it, even though I saw in my mind, with each turning page, which drawing Dimitri was seeing. But I had work to do. One particular job to accomplish tonight. And it was vital the task was completed with success.

I peppered several powders into the can of latex paint, and fuck me for having dropped an entire solo cup of fire engine red tempera on the floor at my feet. I cringed at the loss for a brief second but assured myself it was for the right cause and went back to the subtask. A few more scoops of a teal into the red mixture to get the blue hue in there, then I closed the lid on it. "Dimitri? Could you take this can and buckle it up on the mixer for me?"

"Sure," the halfhearted sound of his response captured my attention and I looked up just as he was sliding my hide-a-sketch pad back under the sofa. That one sliced through me sharper than the loss of paint on my floor. A loss I couldn't put into perspective or into a cause that made it all right. It was just a loss.

I chewed at my lip and let out a heavy sigh to dispel the feeling. No sense grieving. I had things to do. And just as Dimitri came around the work table, I took a wide side step and pulled my padawan to stand right inside the target zone. He never even noticed. I handed the can over to him and forced on a smile to counter those sad puppy eyes that struggled to look up at me.

"You needn't feel sorry for me." But I could see he didn't believe me.

He took the can and walked away toward the back— leaving a trail of bright red footprints behind. And that made my smile brighten to something less forced. Before Dimitri could catch me *red-handed,* I grabbed a roll of brown paper and let it loose over the floor— and over the red trail. Next in the endeavor was the use of a dust broom. I placed a foot on the paper to prevent it from moving so I could swiped the terry cloth broom over the unraveled paper. Once finished, I quickly rolled the paper with the transferred footprint back onto the cardboard tube and stuffed it away.

Step one of *Project Runway*— in stealth mode, no less— was complete.

PORTRAIT SEVENTEEN

DIMITRI CHARMING

Dimitri walked down the hall, peeking through the windows to each studio until he found the person he was looking for. He let out a sigh of determined relief as his timing could not have been more perfect. The choreographer was counting out a few steps as the dancers stood back, catching up on water as they watched.

Dimitri chewed at his lip. It was now or never, and his best friend deserved to have his side defended. He sucked in a deep breath, straightened up his shoulders, and pushed the door open. *No stopping now.*

He marched right across the room between the dancers until he was face to face with Sreven, then drew his hand back and let it fly.

The slap rang out with as much bravado as the sting that lit up in his palm. And it took just as much energy to not let anyone see him or his stung palm quiver.

Sreven's head hardly pitched around, and Dimitri considered repeating it, but then he saw the imprint of fingers start to redden on Sreven's face as he reached up to rub his cheek.

A few of the other dancers started for Dimitri, but Sreven's arm went out to barricade them and he glanced down at Dimitri with the unspoken question.

"Don't fuck it all up like that!" Dimitri was near shaking. He felt the sting of tears in his eyes. He felt every ounce of pain Xherdan had tried to hide. But he had seen the sketches. He saw what no one else saw— what the man was capable of. Xherdan's hands had made love to Sreven on every sheet of pressed paper, then cried and screamed after the break up. The last sketch had said as much, showing a boy hunched over in a squatted position, with arms and hands encapsulating a man's head. Muscles rippled over the back and strained in the legs. The man in the drawing ached and cried. And it had broken Dimitri's heart because the last drawing wasn't of Sreven, it was a self-portrait of Xherdan himself.

"I didn't do this."

"Yes, you did."

"I did not. I found that guy in his warehouse."

"Funny, because I just stopped by the Pumping Station last night and they said you still work there. So where do you get off thinking Xherdan has to stop what he does while you continue to strip for every cornball in the city?"

"I don't want to be second best to his muse."

"A muse isn't a person or something to be jealous of. A muse is an artist's passion. It's the passion that makes a writer able to take ordinary words and put them together to make a reader cry or laugh. It's passion that makes Xherdan take the world and make it more colorful and powerful. It's the same passion that made you dance that day at Studio Hall and how you launched up and did that jump the way you did. Passions aren't something you get jealous over."

"You saw me at the tryouts?" Sreven shook his head in surprise. "How?"

"Xherdan asked one of the guards we work with to pull some strings. So, someone snuck us in."

"He saw me dance? I don't understand then, why does—"

"Because you were too busy fucking up. You let yourself get jealous over his muse. Never come between an artist and his passion. Especially if you ever get to be lucky enough to have one become passionate about you."

"What makes you think he is?"

"You needed only to look at his art work to know that." Dimitri straightened, throwing his chin in the air, more to prevent the tears of anguish from escaping. He turned and marched out in much the same way he'd gone in.

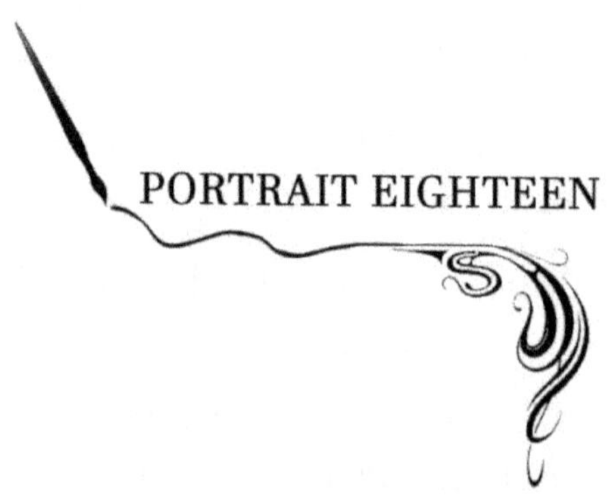

PORTRAIT EIGHTEEN

SREVEN MAQUE

Sreven sat at the bar, fingering his glass, debating on whether or not he should just go ahead and get drunk. Behind him, Jeremy and Kent were dancing out their leather teddy bear number that always got the guys in the audience worked up and excited. But Sreven felt like shit from the heavy storm of rebellious thoughts, stubborn emotions, and his bitching roommate's input. *Just throw it all into a cocktail of heartbreak, add a garnish, and then just keep them coming.*

He'd played that day out over and over in his head, coming upstairs, and seeing that guy all buffed and long black wavy hair with a carpet of chest fur that matched perfectly. He'd nearly lost his cool right away, only the lighthearted kiss from Xherdan had stopped him. But it hadn't been enough to cool him off. And then, when Xherdan handed him the camera and he flipped through image after image of the model-worthy body fondling himself, it had been too much.

He thought for sure Xherdan would have apologized or made up some lame fairy tale that it didn't mean anything. He did none of those. He actually reacted as if Sreven had misplaced his own logic to argue something was red when it was actually white.

He missed him. Missed that quirky ass-ism Xherdan claimed to have. If Xherdan was the epitome of what an ass was, then assholes around the world were getting a bad rep. That or the cat was out of the bag. The cover up revealed, because Xherdan had always felt right all the way up to that day.

"You gonna drink that or nurse it back to health?"

Sreven scowled at Zane, then turned the high ball up and drained it before setting it back down and sliding it over for a refill.

Zane quirked up an eyebrow at him then grabbed the Jim Beam and tipped it over until the glass was full once more.

"Lenny still giving you shit about leaving?"

Sreven grimaced and shook his head. "No." He took a long drink of the bourbon and orange juice, letting it burn his palate to match everything else that ached inside him.

"You didn't get kicked off that dance thing, did you?"

"No, it's still on."

"Then what has you making happy with Mr. Beam?"

"Xherdan."

"I can think of many happier things to make with that man. Let me know if you two want a third to come over and help. I'd be happy to oblige."

"We broke up."

Zane came to a complete stop in his never ending multitasking behind the bar and looked at Sreven. "Luckiest man in New York City and you broke up with him? Got new dance shoes and now you're too good for him? Is that what you're thinking?"

"No, it's not like that."

"Then what is it like?"

Sreven slammed his elbows on the bar then face-planted into his hands. He raked his fingers over the short tendrils of hair he'd carelessly let grow out. "I couldn't trust him. All those guys always wanted to come over and model for him, I can't be at his place twenty-four-seven, and who's to say what goes on half the time. And— dammit, that painter artist mumbo jumbo." But even as he said it he didn't believe it, because he *had* been there. It hadn't been like that at all. Just his roommate Trevor's words chirping in his ear again. Then again, Trevor hadn't been very supportive since the day Sreven had come home from Xherdan's place with a glowing grin and a well-fucked ass.

"Are you sure we're talking about the same guy? I mean, I thought you were dating Xherdan Chantal. Kinda tall, blackish hair, and sexy-as-fuck scruffy face?"

Sreven barely nodded.

"Okay, I can get wanting to make sure your territory is well marked and all, but I don't think the micromanagement stuff is, or was, necessary, was it?"

"No." Sreven confessed, "Being with him was so fucking easy and just felt right all the time." *Too right.* "He snuck inside the studio to watch me try out at that fucking thing. I never even knew until today. He was there, waiting for me afterwards with a picnic basket, and we went out into the park." He shook his head and let out a painful laugh, "Cheesiest date I ever had and I loved every minute of it."

"Picnic basket?" Zane gave him a funny look.

"He's such a damn enigma." Sreven slumped again then downed the rest of his glass.

"What did you just say?"

"Xherdan. He's an enigma."

"If that's true, then why the hell are you treating him like he's just like all the others?"

"What do you mean?"

"You just said he's an enigma."

"Yeah?"

"Yeah, well, you're acting like he treated you like any other asshat that comes in here treats you." Zane grabbed a bar towel and started wiping the counter down, then spun out fresh napkins to the two guys walking up, "Dude, get your ass on straight. THIS—" Zane spread his arms out wide and turned from one side to the other to wave up a display suggesting Sreven to take a good hard look of the club around them, "This is a fucking shithole strip joint. Nothing more." Without interruption, Zane's mind registered the drink orders from the new arrivals and started mixing them up while still berating Sreven for being the idiot in the bunch. "There is no such thing as being a famous stripper, there is no such thing as loving 'being here'. If Xherdan even showed a half an interest in you, you were a fool to fuck it up. He doesn't come here to hook up. None of us has ever known him to get involved with anyone. And that right there says he's a no-drama partner. If it'd been me, I'd be over there right now trying to fix shit. On my knees sucking his cock, and saying sorry while hoping he was falling in love with my ass."

"Why?"

"People don't really wish for themselves to be alone for the rest of their lives. Just some of us are better at waiting for the right one. Like maybe Xherdan. If he is an enigma, then you need to stop acting like someone who's been cheated on."

"But what if I have?"

"You're joking, right?"

Sreven's expression drooped. He hadn't been joking.

"You've been here for all of what, five or six months? Xherdan has been dropping by for maybe two years now. I don't know a single guy he's slept with. And several have tried. Hell, even I was in line waiting for that door to open. Dude is fucking hot, I'd go bottom for him in a heartbeat."

Sreven's shoulders slumped. Letting what Zane said sink in and then he remembered. The near empty, condom box with an expired date on it. It'd been in the bathroom. *Not* next to the bed. *Shit.* He let his head hang. It was just more shit to weigh on him on how much he had fucked it all up. "Well, it's too late then."

"Why's that?"

"I leave in two weeks to join that performance team. He's not going to want to hook up, only for me to leave for seven months in Paris, then another four and a half months out on tour."

"Gotta come back home at some point. At least invite him to the party so you can tell him you're stupid *and* sorry and so he can say goodbye."

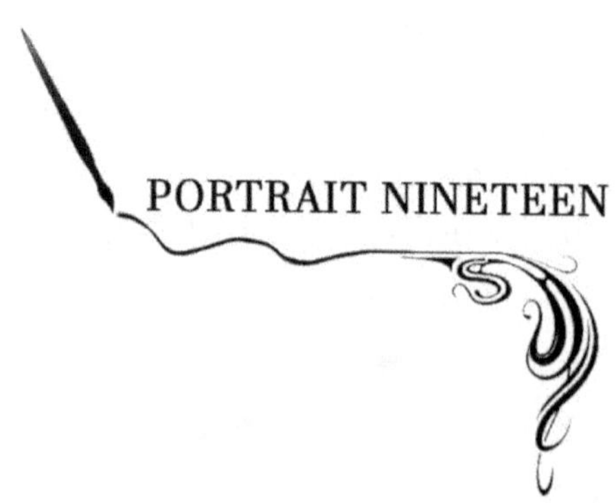

PORTRAIT NINETEEN

I found myself at the Pumping Station, getting the usual pat down from David before going in. But unlike any other time, I had no jokes for him. The whole thing seemed invasive to the point it annoyed me. I felt violated by the contact. It was as if everyone knew Sreven and I were no longer together and now they wanted to get in on the vacant action. *Cop a feel, see if they can climb higher on the ladder of Xherdan.* Of course, none of it was true, and David had gotten his palm jollies off me long before Sreven was a vaulter on my body, so there was no cause for it to be any different. The difference was in me.

Even once inside, I felt out of sorts and broke my habits at every turn. I sat at the bar, watching Zane mix up an order of drinks, and I kept my back to the stage. I didn't want to look. Either it would be him and I wouldn't know what to do with myself— or— it wouldn't be him and I wouldn't know what to do with myself.

Conundrums suck, by the way. They really do. They're worse than misplacing my cool. For with conundrums, not even a pair of rose-colored lenses could mask my lack of indifference. And no amount of plotting was going to help me when in the debacle of it.

"Sreven's not here, by the way." Zane took the liberty to inform me as he set the martini onto a napkin. He must be some kindred spirit to Dimitri, sharing worthless tidbits of trivia I didn't ask for, and sure I would fare better without knowing as well.

At least that settled one dispute for the stage; it wouldn't be *him* on it, therefore I had no desire to look.

I dropped an elbow on the bar and surrendered the bridge of my nose to my fingers, pinching the headache that threatened to haunt my evening. *What the fuck was I going to do with myself?*

Well, for starters, I bottomed my martini and slid it across for another. Zane took the glass, gave me a new one in a matter of minutes, and I bottomed that one too. He looked at me and then at the empty glass, or rather at my hand that kept turning the glass this way then that because it wasn't right. It was empty, which meant it needed to be filled or I needed to go. Two was always the limit, but then again, I was breaking the rules the second I walked in here, and I wasn't making any moves to leave. Either way, so long as the glass was empty, it was misaligned in the universe and I had to keep turning it to try to fix it.

"Okay, just stop." Zane snatched the glass from my hand, "I'll make you another." And I nodded my appreciation before I receded into wayward wandering brooding. If only I could disengage with them. Then I could go back to being the happy ass I was meant to be.

Behind me, the music set changed, a new wave of hooting and yee-haws shouted out from both audience and entertainer. *Must have been the round 'em up cowboy act. God, that one was getting old,* I thought as I finished off another round of stuffy, poisonous liquid.

"Why don't you try talking to him instead?" Zane suggested as he slid my fourth martini in front of me.

"I did."

"When?"

"Tonight, only he's not here, so it's not looking very productive," I begrudged the man a taste of my foul mood, then turned up my glass and drank the evil swill down in one long gulp.

"Did you hear he got a call for a dance gig?"

I sucked in a deep breath and looked at my bartender for once. Why was it that such good news hurt? I bit back something. Fuck, if I understood what painful strife ripped through me at that moment, but it wasn't going to be here that I would give it an audience at my expense, and I managed to force out a congratulatory nod, "That's good. He's a spectacular dancer."

"Even diamonds come from the dirt."

I chewed my lip a moment to picture the rough clear stone trying its best to twinkle and capture an eye from its gravesite deep in the ground. "Yes, yes they do," I muttered finally and slid my glass over for another. "So, who with?"

Zane frowned at my glass but scooped it up anyways, then gave me a shrug. "Some performance dude that likes to mix circus hanging stuff with dance. He leaves for rehearsals in Paris soon."

"Paris?" My attention snapped up in shock with this continuing information. "Why Paris?"

"That's where this producer dude lives or works. Or something. I don't know, but they have to practice for— like, six or seven months, then they're going out on the road. Full production tour, I hear." He set a new drink down in front of me. "We're throwing a farewell party for him. You should come."

"Here?"

"No, boss is holding it at his place. He's got a penthouse over in Soho."

I fell quiet after that. Not sure what to say. Did people actually have responses to such news? If so, what were they? Were there classes one could sign up for to learn? Was I supposed to be angry and wish him a broken leg so he would end up back here where I could find him? Or be happy for him? After all, I did push him to go for the tryouts, what else did I expect to be the results of such support?

Sreven had blown me away that day he danced on the stage. It would only make logical sense that he caught the eyes of someone else, too.

After my sixth martini, Zane cut me off. No sense staying after that, the glass would drive me insane if that hadn't already happened. I sat there a moment longer, fingers tapping on the counter with the fifty in my hand, waiting while Zane was chin deep in a conversation on the phone next to his register.

You ever got that feeling when someone near you was on the phone, or perhaps on the subway, and the couple sitting across from you were talking, but it wasn't English, and after a bit you started to wonder if they were talking about you? Even the vaguest notion of their eyes glancing your way sealed the deal. And that was all it took— a fraction of a glance from Zane and what sounded like a comment about *get down here* and *he's a mess*. I was full on, having one of those insecure Dimitri paranoid moments when I slid the bill across the bar and walked out.

New York City and not a cab in sight. *What was the luck?* None, I supposed as I swayed on my feet and sucked in a noxious lung full of city air. Vacation. That's what I needed. I'd stayed too long and needed to get out. Someplace clean with lots of greenery and flowery colorful stuff. A waterfall would be nice. And just then, I saw the body of a man twirling around a pole that was recessed into the cascading waters of the fall I'd created in my imagination. His arm locked at the elbow, bearing the weight of his body. His torso and legs floating in air with his feet pointed toward the floor and his head thrown back in ecstasy. Once, Sreven even told me the name of the pole dance move. I remember laughing as he rattled off several more moves to me. I was too enthralled just watching him, all grace and strength and— and my hard-on for him. All that blood going to places other than my brain, and I couldn't recite back a single one of those dance step titles.

"Hey, taxi!" David suddenly stepped past me to the curb and hailed down a yellow cab.

The car came to a stop and David held the door open for me.

I sucked in another deep breath. It wasn't anything like what I saw in my head. "Thanks, David," I tried to say without slurring it up too much. I hopped in and gave my driver instructions for the Candy Club with plans to get even drunker.

"Well, if it isn't my not-so-rich prince charming." Bartender boy toy Josh was back behind the bar, much the same way as the last time I saw him there. Only this time, instead of silver shorts, they were camos with the ass bared to all. Just a nice wide black strap from the jockeys that no doubt kept his sock puppet contained up front, also gave his ass that final lift, and perhaps some strap popping fun for those with bigger tips.

"Oh, I'm rich alright. You're just too amateur to know where to look." I matched his acidic sarcasm. I excelled in ass-ism. It was the universal shield from all things uncomfortable and undesirable. I needed it for both, right now.

Josh turned and slung a napkin in front of me, then leaned in, eyes squinting as he studied me. *Truth or dare.* "Bullshit," he husked at me finally.

Dare.

"I live in a twenty-four hundred square foot studio warehouse with a loft space— in New York City. Alone. And I work all of maybe two days a week." I let the asshat grin creep up on my lips. "I call your bullshit."

Oh, the smarts ran slow with this one. He hadn't done the math the first time around. Geometry was the dead giveaway here. In New York, even a piddly seven-hundred-fifty square foot pad could run a couple of grand a month, easy.

Realization made boy toy's eyes grow wide and I felt a hint of *gloatius pigus* in me. "Your sister was right about me. I'm unquestionably rich." I pulled out my wallet and slapped two hundreds on the bar and pushed them towards him, "One's for drinks and the other is to make sure you keep them coming."

Josh was good on the bills, he kept them coming, and I knocked them down until some vague awareness surfaced that it was closing time.

I glanced out the backseat window of a car, watching the city go by. I couldn't even remember having hailed the cab. And only slightly more aware of the arm around my shoulders or the lips that brushed against my neck.

Did you have any idea how much I missed you, I wondered. But then I felt the bristle of a chin and knew right away— *it wasn't you after all who was with me.* However, trying to get my head to surface from that drunk soup I was drowning in, took more strength than perhaps I had.

My mysterious chariot came to a stop and someone was tugging my drunken ass out of the car.

A blur of reddish grey brick made a wall of sliding movement in front of me, and then it wavered, taking me with it in a lean and tilt. A large body caught me and wrangled me upright again. A hand dove into my pockets for my keys, but he was in the wrong one for that. Next, he had my zipper open. I knew because my cock told me it was being invaded by a firm grip. But the scruff of a chin scraped across mine as a tongue slipped past my lips to kiss me. The taste of cheap beer didn't mix well with the martinis that had long since grown stale on my tongue, and I knew it was all wrong.

"Get the fuck off me."

But the hand remained wrapped around my dick and it felt good, whether I wanted it to or not. My head swam with shit I saw that wasn't there, and what *was* there, was spinning. I could hardly grasp where I was or who was actually coming on to me.

It didn't even sound right.

~~Tell me you want me. ~~

But the man with me now, didn't say that. Or anything, other than to ask where my keys were.

I don't want you. And I summoned every atom within me I could gain control over in order to wrench the hand from my pants. "I said get the fuck off of me!"

I felt the hard punch of bricks on my back as Josh shoved me against the wall. I saw stars in the backs of my eyelids, then felt the slide of the wall against my back as I went crashing toward the sidewalk.

"You're just a washed up drunk painter. No wonder your boyfriend left you. You can't even get it up."

"You are so spot on," I laughed wickedly from the sidewalk, not caring I was down there. Not caring what insults boy-toy-bartender tried to bristle me with. I just stayed there, mentally and emotionally trapped in some strange void between laughing and crying, which oddly felt like floating on a raft in rough seas.

I was hardly aware Josh had left until there was a much different face of a much different color staring down at me.

"Say, what up, homey? You got any money on you?" The new arrival leaned down and began patting my pants.

 I only laughed.

"Where the fuck's your money, fool?"

Ironic wasn't it? Being so drunk the street thugs were going to rob me with the casualty of getting the mail. "Bartender has it. How else you think I got drunk, fuckface?"

Guess he didn't like my answer, because the next and last thing I remember was pain stabbing me in the ribs from my would-be mugger's foot, then a large fist coming down over my face. Then it was lights out.

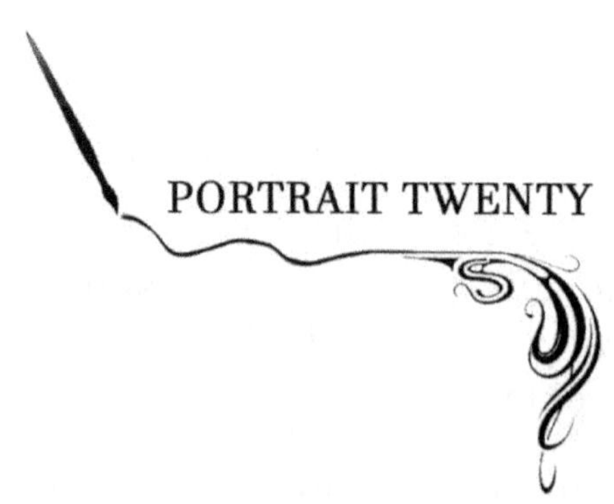

PORTRAIT TWENTY

I woke to the intrusion of someone slapping my face, then blaring sunlight seared past my eyelids to fry my brain.

"Hey, kid." Another smack to my rather tender jaw. "Come on, wake up, kid. You been out for who knows how long."

Its iconic in a way how the simplest thing like an accent and you know just what kind of person or who is your newest company. This sone in particular was pure New York Italian.

I cracked my eyes open, finding the up close and personal face of Louis Fitonnio: *the real,* staring at me. It was far from the wakeup call I'd grown accustomed to, and I squeezed my eyes shut again.

My mouth felt dry as if it'd been stuffed with cotton. I licked my lips, only to regret it when I felt the slicing cut in the corner of my mouth and another on my lip. I finally got my eyes open once more, but the view hadn't gotten any better, "Anyone ever tell you you're ugly?"

"My wife, but right now you ain't no beauty queen yourself." He pulled me up to sitting, which didn't feel like a grand idea at the moment, and I found myself holding my head, wishing I had a bullet for it.

"So what happened to you? You get robbed last night?"

My hands went to my pants pocket on cue and seemingly came up empty, "Guess so." Returning them back to my head again.

"You mean, I actually gotta kill someone now?" the wise ass spoke, "All these years and you gotta blow it for me."

Despite the warning signs going off in my head like a five-alarm fire for a hangover, I glanced around, and that's when the entire earth pitched underneath me, and the wave of nausea sent a choking stomach, full of bile, over the armrest of the sofa.

Turned out, Louis' cousins, Carlo and Mario, were also there, circled around. Mario stepped in and passed a washcloth over for my head.

Little by little, reality and proximity crept back to the present. They had me on the derelict sofa still out on the sidewalk, which had yet to be picked up by the garbage detail. Probably because the guys were always sitting on it. Beat standing when it was smoke-break time.

"Carlo, get the car out and run the kid up to the hospital to have him checked, will ya? And you—" Louis wagged his finger my way. "You call my brother, Franco, down at the precinct to get a report made, then call your credit card peoples, and get the things shut off before whoever mugged you wipes you out."

I nodded. Though preferably, I would have had him take me around back and put me out of my misery.

Two stitches, a headache tea plus four Advils later, I was at work, still wishing Mr. Fitonnio had just taken me around back of the warehouse and put a bullet in my head instead.

I didn't think it could get worse, but lo and behold, I learned I was wrong when I got called up to the front and there stood Sreven.

"Oh shit, what happened?"

I flinched back when Sreven attempted to reach for my face. Once was enough, and I wasn't so sure Sreven was beyond taking a cheap shot to vent his own frustrations. If he had them.

"I'm sorry, I—"

"It's okay, just hurts."

A shadow passed over his face. I should have added *'when I touch it'* to my answer, but I didn't, and now I realized what I *had* said had also hurt him, but I couldn't bring it back.

He nodded. "I, uh, I wanted to come by and give you this." He thrust a cream-colored envelope out at me. I stared at it a moment. Rambling off a list of items I'd heard so many others claimed to have delivered after a break up— annulment papers— restraining orders— *Sorry-I-broke-your-heart* Hallmark card.

"It's an invitation."

Wedding? That would suck.

"The owner of the Station is throwing a party for me."

I nodded, still not saying anything. I was certain Zane ratted me out that I had been there last night and that I was made aware of the news.

"You were right."

"About?"

"About the tryouts and I have only you to thank for it."

"No, I just introduced you to someone I knew. I never expected Alan to give you an audition spot. I just didn't want your night with me to be all about people talking nonsense about my paintings."

He sat back a fraction and gave me a surprised look, "Really? But you made all this happen."

"I didn't make anything happen." I grew agitated. "Like Alan told you, you had to perform the dance."

"Yeah, but you made me go."

"I didn't do that either." I hated getting credit for something I didn't do. They were as empty and meaningless as appraisal for shit you didn't like.

He looked even more hurt then, a slight twitch to his right eye, then somewhere in his head he flipped a switch and the shields went up. It was like watching a glass window scroll up. It might be transparent but you could see it all the same.

"It's a brand new dance concept. The choreographer's name is Derreck Albright. The tour is being sponsored by some company in France, so we're all going there for the rehearsals." His eyes weren't as clear and vibrant as usual. They seemed cloudy like an overcast day seen through the city smog.

I glanced away and tested the split in my lip with a probing tongue as a divergence.

"Rehearsals are seven months, then the tour starts—" the rest fell away. "Sorry, Xherdan. I— I got hurt. I should have trusted you."

I said nothing.

Suddenly, he was thrusting a small box towards my hands. Funny, because I hadn't noticed he'd been holding it.

"What's this?"

He fidgeted. "It's a camera. To replace the one I broke." The antsy footwork continued. "I'm not sure if it's the right one. I couldn't find anyone who knew."

The last bit struck a chord with me and bristled my mood. "In other words, you were trying to find out who I've slept with since."

"No! It's not like that. I didn't— I've never met anyone like you, and it just seemed too good to be true, so I started looking for a flaw. Because even if you're not right for everyone else, you were perfect for me. So, when I saw—" he let out a frustrated sigh of defeat. "I just— I got possessive. I didn't want to lose you and I didn't want to share you with anyone either."

This was probably the moment when I should have said something. Perhaps tell him all was forgiven. That it was a mistake and that it was okay. But as I have been trying to tell you, I'm no good at this. I'd had little to no practice because I was never willing to get involved in practice runs. So— as par for the course of Xherdan Ass-isms— I said nothing.

There was a long, silent pause— plenty of time for me to change my mind, but I couldn't think of anything to say.

"I'm going to miss you terribly."

I dropped my head and stared at the clunky, tactical style black leather boots on his feet. Even in them, I was attracted to the sexy feet in them, but I couldn't let him see that. Not anymore.

"Okay, well, I got to go. I hope you'll come to the party," Sreven fished for something else to say.

Without even glancing up, I nodded, tucked the box under my arm, and watched his boots carry him away, then silently I shoved my hands in my sweater pockets, returned to my work, and to the game of twenty questions from Dimitri.

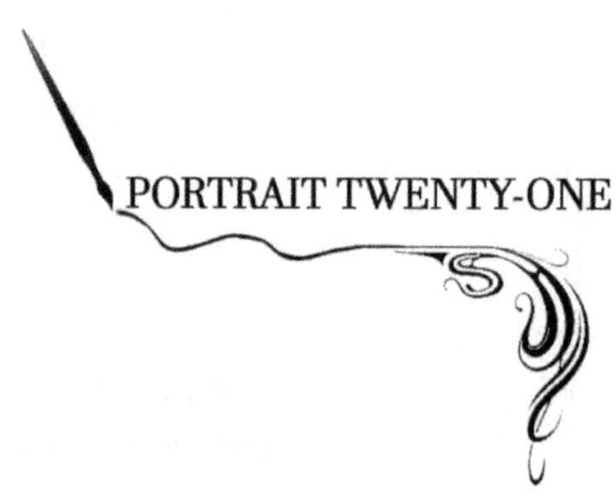

PORTRAIT TWENTY-ONE

I lingered in the back of the room, like any good introvert would. A local band, comprised of a singer, drummer, and two keyboardists, were just starting up a familiar cover tune by Gotye. The music dispelled some of the party hum of conversations while I was soaking up the view of the flirtatious ocean that flooded the room. Bodies that listed and swayed. Hips screaming out with perfunctory wanton to enrapture the attention of far more robust builds. It was sensual yet pandemic of being boorishly overplayed. The large, sculpted, brazen men for topping. The lithe boys for bottoming. Dominant and submissive play-forms—

all neatly tucked away in their proper positions of performance. About the only lively spark it held was when a few of those tenderloin bottoms got bratty because a top had eyes for something else. The friction of competition. Still, the soap opera of seduction was too cliché— too predictable— too empty. *Okay, I came. Can I go home now?*

> *Pick apart— The pieces of your heart—*
> *And let me peer inside—*

Why did I even care? All I wanted for my life was an active muse for my paintings, and every once in a blue moon have one of those beautiful bodies ride my cock to his heart's content so I can remember how its done before sending home.

> *Let me in— Where only your thoughts*
> *have been— Let me occupy your mind—*
> *As you do mine—*

So, what did it matter what everyone else was doing? If it suited them fine, it mattered none for me.

> *Your heart's a mess— You won't admit to it— It makes no sense— But I'm desperate to connect— You can't live like this*

My defiant thoughts froze as the lyrics to the song barged inside my head, refusing to be ignored as I had tried. As the voice that sang them pushed out a crescendo that could give, even the likes of the singer Sting, the chills.

In they seeped and I lost the battle. Now I had to listen.

> *You have lost— (Too much love)— To fear, doubt and distrust— (It's not enough)— You just threw away the key— To your heart—*

A waiter swept by with a tray of assorted drinks, balanced perfectly, and poised over his shoulder which, more importantly, blinded his periphery. A perfect opportunity for me to snatch one rather than to wait. Leaving the luck of my palate to the random landings of universal equations of infinite possibilities, or simply the luck of the draw decided from some eight or so concoctions.

> *You don't get burned— ('Cause nothing*
> *gets through)— It makes it easier—*
> *(Easier on you)— But that much more*
> *difficult for me— To make you see—*

More importantly, it was just something to break my thoughts, keep those words out of my defenses. I didn't need cracks, I needed stimulation.

> *Love ain't fair— So there you are— My*
> *love—*

> *Your heart's a mess— You won't admit*
> *to it— It makes no sense— But I'm*
> *desperate to connect— And you, you*
> *can't live like this—*

And just then, the sea of mundane bodies parted and a familiar body appeared across the room. Those powerful shoulders seen clearly under the form-fitting shirt, not even the cap sleeve hid the contours of his arms. Angled torso and the ass I recalled with too much clarity how well it seated over my loins. He turned, his eyes doing a double take before locking with my gaze.

*Your heart's a mess— You won't admit to
it— It makes no sense— But I'm
desperate to connect— And you can't live
like this—*

The fucking music talking to me— to us—

*Love ain't safe— You won't get hurt if you
stay chaste— So you can wait— But I
don't wanna waste my love—*

The song ended and I wasn't going to hang around to find out what deep wrenching message the universe of fate had to tell me. I turned the high ball up until the ice cubes slammed against my lips and I let the burning whiskey and sweet and sour mixer find its way down my throat. I deposited the glass somewhere along the way as I rushed out the door to make my escape.

"Xherdan!"

I ignored him, tearing down the stairs, and out the door into the city below. Cool damp air greeted me.

*~~But I'm desperate to connect And you
can't live like this.~~*

I wanted to just stop right there and turn my face up to the drizzle that was already coming down. But the song was still preaching in my head and I heard Sreven's tennis shoes coming down much faster than I had. I could run. Yes, I could run.

~~ Your heart's a mess— You won't admit to it— It makes no sense— ~~

And I turned and headed down the sidewalk at a fast pace. I heard the door to the building swing open and his voice call out, "Xherdan!"

~~Your heart's a mess— you won't admit to it— it makes no sense—~~

"But I'm desperate to connect—" I sang under my breath, staring down at my feet as he hurried down the concrete after me.

~~But you can't live like this.~~

Then Sreven caught up with me. The hand of a familiar bossy bottom I'd felt before, grabbed and spun me around, nearly sending me into the building. A pained man glared at me. "Why didn't you stop?"

I shook my head— what a conundrum this was. I kept everything in my life so well organized and planned. I had a plan for everything— a contingency even. Nothing left without preparations of how it would be played out. *Except this.* I didn't even have an answer.

"So, you don't talk to me now either, is that it?"

I forced on a shrug. "You were with someone. I didn't want to interrupt. You know I'm not good com—"

"No, I wasn't with someone," he cut in, shaking his head, and stepped in closer.

I could feel him. Felt his desires, felt the compatibility I had felt before. I dropped my gaze, unsure of myself, just words still rambling in my head.

"But I would very much like to be with you." Sreven ducked down, trying to see into my eyes— eyes I tried to keep hidden.

~~ But I'm desperate to connect.~~

"I— I don't—"

"You don't what? You don't want to be with me?" The hurt heard as much as shown in his expression and his eyes.

"My heart's a mess." Song words I never meant to whisper came out, yet freeing once I did.

"Say you want me." Sreven was suddenly moving in and I fell into his kiss.

My arms being pulled around his body and shoulders. The embrace received in like form, and I just— *did*—

No thinking, just reacting. I simply moved— *no*— I *felt*. Felt Sreven wrapping around me, though it was me encompassing him.

"Just tell me you want me."

"I want you."

"Tell me you want to be inside me."

We worked our way down the brick wall, closing in on the alleyway.

"I want to be inside you," I answered between boughts of drowning in his lips and tasting his tongue. Finding that similar sport drink flavor on it.

I couldn't believe I'd turned into his pet Mynah bird, mimicking the words he told me to say. His head turned one way, then the next, our kiss switching from one embrace to another, consuming us as much as we consumed each other. And then, I saw inside myself what I had been blindly looking away from. A developing emotion I had tried to say I didn't feel. Because until now it had never existed. Now I realized I did.

"I love you," I gasped when we broke to get a breath.

No sooner the words spoken, it all stopped. Our kiss frozen, dead in the moment.

Fucking Shit. I'd fucked up, realizing what I'd just said. That wasn't at all what Sreven wanted me to say. *For Mary's sake, backpedal, you stupid fool.*

I shook my head, brought my hand up between us to create the necessary fissure and wiped at my forehead, "I'm sorry." I shook it off, "I don't know what's come over me. Too much drink and stress I suppose. It was a mistake, Sreven. Really."

"No. You don't make mistakes." Sreven sounded hardened. His hands dropped to his side and mine mirrored him. We stood there squared off like another memory had of us.

Strange. Nature has a way of extenuating a man's moods. I don't know how, but it did, just as it did now. A low rumble rolled overhead that shook inside my chest, then the drizzle that enveloped us like a mist grew heavy and then rain poured down in sheets. Within seconds we were both soaked, just staring at each other, with lust that still heaved in our chests and expelled out with foggy breaths.

"People throw that word around like condoms, roll it on for sex, then discard it just as quickly when it's over," he told me while he futilely wiped the rain from his eyes, even as more dripped from his short hair, down his forehead, and off his brows. It was fascinating and I could see the very image already on one of my tapestries. "But you don't," he added.

"I'm sorry." I didn't even know why I said that. Sorry. Sorry for what? For being a fool and listening to some fucking song?

I closed my eyes and finally there was just darkness. The colors that had spiraled in my head turned every thought into movement and washed away, like the storm runoff rushing down the gutters and vanishing into the drains. Sorry. What a fucking lame word. It had no body, no color, no power of poetry. So, I turned and ran.

"I LOVE YOU TOO!"

It could have been just the voice of the rain trying to trick me, but my feet slodded to a stop and I turned. I had to be sure, for all these uncertainties would plague me for far too long if I didn't.

I hadn't even realized I'd already made it down half the block, but there he was, way up there where I had left him, standing like a demigod whose temples had been destroyed or lost, his subjects fled for drier cover. He looked broken. The sight jabbed me straight to my heart.

"I don't know what it means, but God help me, I do!" he cried out.

Xherdan, you fool, you know perfectly well that two backpedals puts you right back where you started.

But that was precisely where I wanted to be.

I rushed back to him, nearly colliding into his arms as he fell into mine. Maybe it was desperation, but it felt utterly foreign. A little scary, but warmly refreshing.

"Tell me you love me again," he demanded between interchanged kisses.

"Bossy little bottom, you are."

His arms snaked up around my shoulders and back, encompassing me, clinging to me, holding me, telling me he wasn't going to let go until I did. "Tell me."

"I love you."

"I love you, too." He smiled against my lips.

We didn't bother talking any more. How does one top those words other than to make love in the rain in a dirty alley? But as raunchy as one might think, for me it was brilliantly amazing in a cascade of new colors.

PORTRAIT TWENTY-TWO

I don't think Sreven even went back upstairs to say goodbye to the friends who'd gathered to send him off onto the new journey of his life. At least, I couldn't recall it. We'd made love in that alley, up until the point we realized neither of us had a condom with us. No surprise on my part and perhaps not for him either. We almost let it slip as an act of trust, but at the last minute we decided we didn't want to risk ourselves to foolish mistakes or haste, so it was an act of hands and kissing. Though not with a sliver of connection lost between us.

After a nefarious ally frotting. We caught a cab back to my place, Sreven leaning back against me the whole trip, and we only laughed that the cap driver blamed us for ruining his seats being as sodden as we were.

I remember running my fingers over Sreven's short hair and kissing the top of his head, but anything logical, like house keys, or paying the cab were void from my memory like they never happened.

Fleeting glimpses of making love to each other's body with towels and nothing more before climbing in bed.

Now we were curled into each other's arms under the covers listening to the rain that continued outside, rapping on the tin sheeting of rooftop features above the loft— safe, content, and sated.

"Come away with me," he whispered in the darkness of the loft.

I kissed the top of his head, regretting my answer before I ever even said it, "I can't, my work is here, my home, my paintings."

"You can paint in Paris, too. Just think, we can walk down the halls of the Louvre after dinner, go kiss on one of the bridges. You can't tell me you wouldn't enjoy it there."

I wrapped around him, to test if it were possible I could pull him any closer to me than I already had him. We were far from a clean and mannerly spooning. Rather, our legs were tangled about each other, I had one arm over his shoulder, embracing him across his chest, the other around his side. His was as equally latched on, reaching over his head and behind my neck, playing with the strands of hair that had begun to get long. He had his other hand reaching behind him, clutching at my waist, and his head resting back on my chest, partially tucked under my chin.

You wouldn't have thought it to be comfy from the looks of our awkward placement of limbs, but I don't think I could have been more so. He just fit against me in every way imaginable. That's when I realized it. Something was about to put one very painful crack across the beautiful new marble.

They always say when water gets into those cracks, it's over.

PORTRAIT TWENTY-THREE

How many weeks had it been now? One— two— three—? I stepped back once I jumped off the scissor lift.

It was finished.

The final masterpiece to replace the one I had destroyed. Though— I glanced at it, tucked away in the far back corner of the studio— I hadn't had the heart to do away with it. We'd made love on that canvas. Spilled our semen into the wet paint. I couldn't part with it.

But now, I had something new. A moment frozen for eternity. Not the base debauchery we'd shared in the other. This one had passed between us and no one knew it. No one but me and my Muse.

I should have seen it coming. But I didn't because I am such an ass, and the next thing I knew the tears were streaming down my cheeks with my heart aching and my chest threatening to crack open. A guy just couldn't figure when lust turned to love. Fuck, love hurt and sucked.

How did it ever come to this? Why should love be wasted upon the inverts of artistic expression? We should be nothing but witnesses to the spectacle so that we can paint, play or sculpt it. But we should never have to suffer what it feels like, because what I felt just then betrayed all the glorious images I had swathed over my white stages.

I walked around the forest— no longer blank white faces towering over me. Now they were galaxies of chaos and color; and hidden within each of them were the secret gardens of the physique of men.

I had ten large canvases all finished now. And dotted around them, like shrubbery, were framed paper with my sketches. However, none stood as grand as the one of Mikhail Baryshnikov.

The renounced dancer captured, standing idly in his rehearsal garbs, hand on the back of a wicker chair, and one foot crossed behind his other leg, propped on toes. His attention looking off toward something offstage. He was the first man I had ever loved.

I walked up front to the brand-new easel with its blank new sketch paper. It was the exact same size as Mikhail's was. Delivered just this morning. I looked over the white, rough surface, already in love with its purpose. I had one more sketch to do and the collection would be finished. But first, I had one last thing to do at the Metropolitan.

"You're not giving me a whole lot of room to work with you on this, Xherdan. I like you and we've been very happy with you here at the Metro, but I have a museum to run, and it takes a particular amount of staff to do that." Renaud sat back in his chair behind his desk with his hands folded over his lap. The wall behind him was lined with dark wood shelves, heavy with books of nearly every art and artifact one might dream or wonder about. One could have spent as much time, or maybe even more, exploring the wonders of his private office as one might have spent browsing the whole of the Metro. *I was really going to miss it here.*

"I understand." I kept smiling. "It was just as sudden for me too. That's why I tried to come up with a recommendation for my replacement. Lita Underwood would work well with Dimitri Charming. She knows her art work and could use the experience to complete her degree at school."

"This isn't a revolving door job, Xherdan. You're asking me to hire someone, then kick them back out when you return."

"Lita wishes to return home after she finishes her school. I'll be back long before her last semester ends."

"I don't know. This is highly unorthodox. You are aware of this, are you not?"

"Yes, I understand. It's the best recommendation I can offer to help fill the museum's needs due to my sudden leave of absence."

He rocked in his chair, contemplating me for a long moment. "What happens if I can't do this?"

I smiled and nodded to him. "I'm going to miss this place." I glanced around, admiring the couple of pieces Renaud kept to himself in his office. "I really enjoyed working here. It's held a special place in my heart for the better part of my life, but I have to do this."

"Well, Xherdan, I can't promise things will work out in your favor here at the Metropolitan, but I wish you the greatest of experiences and adventures on your journey."

"Thank you, sir." The warmth and happiness I felt within my own smile said it was going to be one of those milestone selfie days.

ONE LAST APERÇU

DIMITRI CHARMING

When he arrived, Dimitri came around front to the security desk as called.

Since Xherdan had left on his seven-month leave to be with his lover in Paris during the rehearsal months, Dimitri had found it hard to stay focused on the job or on his own artwork. Even dancing seemed to be less thrilling. Life was just hard without his best friend and role model there to keep his chin up.

"Hey, Ramone, you rang?"

"Sure did." He stood up, reaching under the counter and produced several gift-wrapped boxes, set them on the counter, and pushed them toward Dimitri. Each wrapped in shiny foil and topped with glittery ribbons and bows.

Dimitri felt the sides of his mouth twitching with the threat of a smile. "What is this?"

"Special delivery for you. Said for you to open them right away." Ramone waved the courier's slip in his hand.

"Hey, don't forget this?" Bert was bending over to grab something then suddenly produced a glossy gift bag and set it next to the wrapped boxes.

"Oh, right, right. Thanks, Bert." The grin said it all.

They were up to something, but Dimitri couldn't hold back the wave of excitement either. Someone had sent him a present.

He pulled the bag to him first and peeked in, his eyes widening as he reached in and pulled— and pulled a little more until finally the long swath of sheer Chartreuse and Pale Rose dip-dyed scarf fell free from the bag. Dimitri felt his eyes bug out, right along with the warm feeling rise in his cheeks. He didn't even wait before wrapping it loosely around his neck several times, then let the ends fall down his sides, one in front of the other and then tossed back over his shoulder.

"Looks damn good on you, Dimi."

Dimitri felt a rising in the flutter and quickly tore into the first box to see what else he had gotten. He blushed a bit as Ramone and Bert's eyes grew just as wide as his had as a pair of black and multi-neon-colored splattered lycra-style pants came into view. The funny thing was, the print on them looked a lot like one of Xherdan's paintings translated onto fabric.

Closer inspection revealed a few boxy shapes had been cut out and replaced with black mesh to show off a bit of skin around a hipbone and the opposite thigh. The final embellishment was the designer's name on the black waistband: Marco Marco.

The next box, when unraveled, was a finely crafted wooden box. The kind one would expect to have secrets or magical trinkets hidden inside. But, in fact, what it did hold was even more spectacular as Dimitri opened it up and stared at the collection of color pastel pencils. A card inside read: "Do what you do best. Like you said, the others are already taken, so work on being you."

Tears pooled in Dimitri's eyes and he quickly swiped them away with the backs of his fingers. He couldn't cry right now; he had to open the next present to see what it was.

He didn't even slow down for ceremony, just tore through the foil and popped the top of the shoe box off, and that's when the foyer filled with the high shriek that had both Ramone and Bert wiggling fingers in their ears.

Dimitri jumped back, both hands clapped over his mouth, and tears returning to stream down his cheeks like tiny rivers. His face felt so hot it had to have turned beyond any pink shade.

With his feet frozen to the floor, he reached out, barely touched the shoes inside before snapping his fingers back. They were real.

He leaned towards them again. This time, a little less afraid that it was just a dream.

He slipped his slender fingers under the high arch of one shoe, caressing the red sole, and along the spiked heel. Then, with both hands, he thrust into the box and pulled them out. More tears streamed freely as he hugged the black platform high heels, with the red soles, to his heart. *Fucking asshole had bought him Christian Louboutins.*

"Well? You gonna try them on?" Bert asked with a grin.

Dimitri glanced around, half fearing there might be someone else around, and when his eyes assured them there wasn't, he glanced back at the guys and twirled his finger, silently commanding them to turn around.

They both chucked.

"Yeah, alright," Ramone agreed and he and Bert both stood and turned their backs to him while Dimitri dropped his pants right there to change them out for the new designer digs. They fit just as Lycra was meant to fit, but *oooohhhhhhh* his inner Diva was shouting *hallelujah!* Because it was more than just designer tights— it was a transformation. Like when the girls put on the Fire Engine Red lipstick. However, his gear needed a bit of basket adjusting, and finally Dimitri redressed his new over flowing scarf, along with his shirt, so they hung down to hide his goods a little better, not wanting to get too carried away with letting his diva down-there bits shaped out. Next, were the shoes. *Was there such a thing as chocolate for feet?*

Because that's what Louboutins felt like. How the hell had Xherdan managed to send a pair that fit so perfectly?

Dimitri walked around in circles just loving the *click click* sound on the marble floor as it echoed in the open foyer— feeling seven inches taller. He came back around to where Ramone and Bert were watching him. Only Dimitri couldn't hide his inner beaming any longer.

The open and shut of a door echoed from down the hall, followed by approaching footsteps. Ramone grabbed the boxes, shoved them back under the desk station, and Dimitri tossed his pants over the counter to be stashed away with the boxes.

Bert jutted his chin over to the side to give a silent *get out of here.*

"Thanks, guys." And he took off— no— he catwalked away— like he owned the place.

"Looking good, Dimitri Charming," Ramone called out to him.

Only, Dimitri-diva wasn't about to look over his shoulder and let them see how much the flattery affected him.

Dimitri walked along the dim halls of the museum. He'd finished the display of First-Century Roman Mold-blown glass by the master glassworker Ennion and could finally call it a night. He took the long way around towards the break room, wanting to pass through the latest works that had just arrived last week.

He soon turned down the great hall and the dim world was transformed into a kaleidoscope of brilliant colors. Displayed on wall-sized paintings where splashes and blurs of every color in an eclectic motion frozen on each and every canvas.

The first, one of his favorites, was a set of three curled trumpet flowers in the likeness of calla lilies that stood nearly five feet each, one lone flower per canvas. Hidden along their forms were the profiles of a man's side, the masculine hand clearly defined by subtle shades of gray paint, cleverly concealed in the colors and contours of the flower, but all easily capturing the eye. It was masculine and feminine married with vivid colors and shadow.

Those that followed all had a familiar beauty of color in an out-of-control way, as though the rainbows in the sky came crashing down in paints to coat the earth in ecstasy. Like the one with the flowers, each held a hidden physique molded in perfection. Sometimes the admirers had to look for them, but once you did, there was no losing the genius of the art. So powerful and enlightening. There was no way to feel sad when the waterfalls of color encompassed the room.

Dimitri had walked between them every night since their arrival. They made him feel so good, he'd begun wearing his heels to work, dressing like he'd just stepped off a catwalk. He felt empowered to be free that way.

He even let his hips sway in an exaggerated swish— prissing like he owned the place until he came to the centerpiece of the exhibit. It stood from floor to near the maximum allowance. Which in here was twelve feet. And it was wider than if Dimitri stood with his arms stretched out to his sides— twice. It was truly Xherdan's masterpiece and it would also be returning, after the tour was over, to become a permanent resident in the museum. The body of the pole dancer gripped the pole between just one arm in an elbow lock and a shoulder. The dancer's head and free arm thrown back in a pose of finality, while the powerful dancer arched his back, so that his toes pointed straight down towards the floor. The entire physique was in gray scale laid over a sea of splashing rainbow. To say it was beautiful was a disservice of the English language; it was much more. An adoration for an art, only a lover and poet— or perhaps a talented painter— could ever express.

And expressed it well, he had.

But it was still not Dimitri's favorite-favorite. Rather, that was the two, six-foot life-size charcoal sketches just next to the masterpiece. One a was of the famous Russian ballet dancer, Mikhail Baryshnikov. The moment sketched out in timeless pause, perhaps in a rehearsal hall with a hand propped on a lute while he looked off stage.

The second drawing, made to create a set of the two, captured another man standing similarly. But unlike Mikhail, this one who looked extraordinarily like Sreven Maque looking directly at the viewer wearing practice tights and drooping leg warmers and chalked guards wrapping only the balls of his feet. The starting hints of some deeply warm expression on his face that was just starting to brighten, as if someone he loved had just walked into the studio to surprise him.

So life-like, it was easy to imagine the dancer was actually standing there, face to face, alive and in person.

The information card that sat on a small podium with them read:

> ~~*"My Past and My Future. The only two loves in my life. One, when I was far too young to possess, but possessed me so completely that he would not be replaced until another heart-touching dancer leaped into my life. Only this one would forever stay my happy ever after."* ~ *Renowned Painter and Artist, Xherdan Chantal* ~~

Dimitri let out a dreamy sigh, then made a *waltzey* turn, and swished off— turning the display lights off on his way out.

THE END

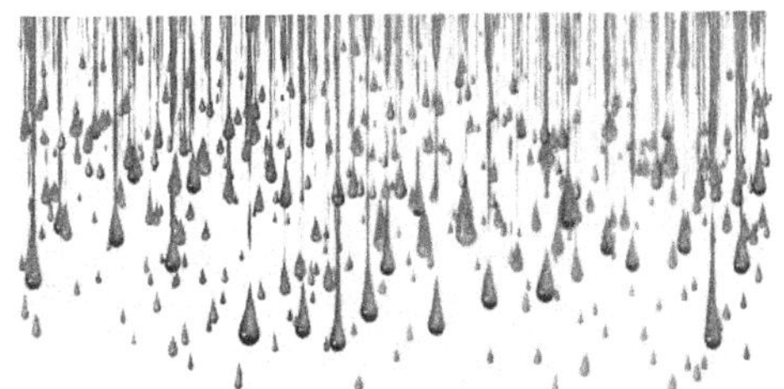

BONUS

ARTWORK BY TARIAN P.S.

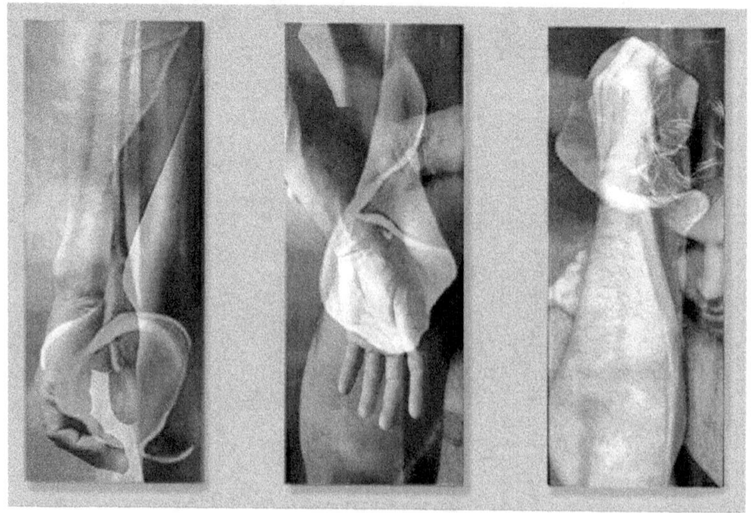

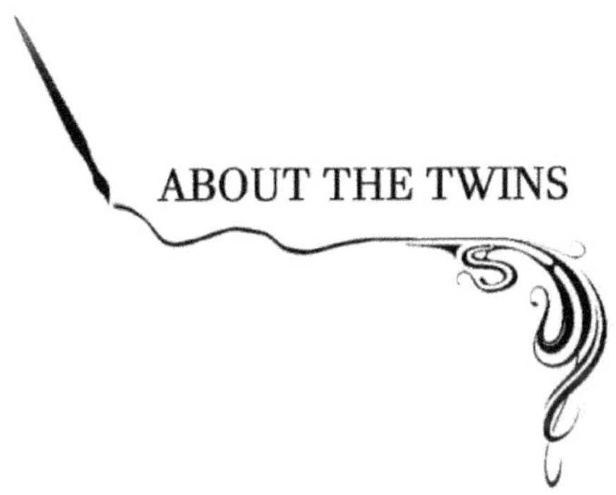

ABOUT THE TWINS

Both Proud Indy Authors: Tarian like his twin, Talon, love to torment their editor with a nefarious world of Archaic words, foreign-language, slang, colloquialism of cultural local dialect, stretched/outside-of-the-box definitions, and have even been known to throw in some new word construct creations of their own at times. This, of course, is all thrown in there with the dyslexia soup stock they both suffer from that makes editing for them a joy *{joy: n. see mental illness}*.

However, the final product comes out as richly detailed as we believe all stories should be created: holographic worlds of love, pain, frustration, and challenges beyond the every day. We believe a good story should take you on an emotional ride, pluck your heart strings, and zing you about until you're dizzy and screaming at the antagonist, while cheering for the protagonist before returning you to your cozy reading spot. And we've created these adventures within a mix of genres, so you can find the one right for you: Gay & Het Romances, Suspense, Paranormal and Sci-fi Erotic Romances, War-time Romance Fictions, along with Talon's favorites of Erotica and Space-Sci-Fi Frontiers, and Tarian's favorite works of Post-Apocalyptic Dark Fantasies and Historical Fantasies— all for readers to submerse themselves into, and escape, from their day when they need or desire, and to whet your appetite for more.

Because in the end— *oh the places we will go.*

"A true Storyteller does not deliver a product,
they deliver an experience." ~ Author Tarian P.S.
TALON PS &
TARIAN PS

DISCOVER THESE OTHER TITLES BY
TALON PS & TARIAN PS

DOMINION OF BROTHERS SERIES
Becoming His Slave
Domming the Heiress
A Place for Cliff
Rough Attraction
Taking Over Trofim
Right One 4 Diesel
Touching Vida~Vince

LA SERIE DES FRERES DU DOMINION – (French Edition)
Devenir Son Esclave - Partie 1 & 2
Dominer l'Heritiere
Un Havre pour Cliff
Attirance Brutale

QUANTUM MATES:
Pt 1~ What Torin Wants

DEAR SOLDIER SERIES:
Dear Soldier, With Love
Dear Soldier, With Love II: A Lost Soldier Named Grey

❦

LYCOTHARIAN COLLECTION:
Bond of the Lycaon Concubine

❦

TALON's KEEP COLLECTION:
Feral Dream by Talon PS
Danny's Dom by Nick Hasse

❦

Three Wrong Turns

❦

Muse Me Only
Inspire Moi Seulement (French Edition)

❦

That's My Ethan

❦

THE TEDDY BEAR COLLECTION:
Their Plane from Nowhere
Big Spoon & Teddy Bear
Ivan vs Ivan
TIME: Wounds All Heal
Shaggin' the Dead

❦

THE SADOU ORDER – A Dark Taboo Series
Perfect Boy / Perfect Son

THE PENDHRAGAIN LEGENDS
A Pre-Arthurian Historical Fantasy
Anáil Dhragain (Dragon's Breath)

KEEPERS OF DESTINY SERIES
A Post-Apocalyptic Dark Fantasy
Keeping With Destiny

TOPAZ OF ARABIA AND HER FOREVER HOME JOURNEY
A Safe For All Ages Coloring / Activity Books

THE ADVENTURES OF HUGH JORGAN
as ROCK HARDING ~ An Adult Naughty Coloring Books

CONNECT AND FOLLOW THE TWINS:

WWW.TALON-PS.COM